HOT ASH
and the
Oasis
Defect

PHILIP WYETH

This is a work of fiction. Names, characters, places, and incidents either are the product of the author's imagination or are used fictitiously, and any resemblance to actual persons, living or dead, events, or locales is entirely coincidental.

Also by this author:
Reparations USA
Reparations Mind
Reparations Core
Chasing the Best Days

The author would like to express his gratitude to the friends and family who have offered encouragement over the past two years. Special thanks to David, Bryan, Brigitte, Jason, and Geff for their insights and enthusiasm during the writing of this book.

Note to Readers: This book contains adult language and sexual themes.

Cover design by Philip Wyeth.

www.philipwyeth.com
www.oasisdefect.com

CONTENTS

1. Duty Calls 1

2. Girls' Night Out 7

3. A New Malaise 13

4. The Night is Female 17

5. Ecstasy 27

6. Scene of the Crime 34

7. Game Room 49

8. Dionysian Nights 54

9. Dead on the Sidewalk 70

10. That Human Touch 80

11. Arms Race of Chaos 89

12. Just Like That 95

13. Roller Coaster 101

14. Her Melon Scent 113

15. Tasty Trader 122

16. Score One for the Runts 125

17. That Fragile Truce 129

18. Intuition 135

19. Rules of the House 139

20. Her Ultimate Fear 144

21. Unhealthy Desires 149

22. Inexhaustible Hate 155

23. Live Bait 162

24. Spilling His Guts 168

25. A Million Naughty Elephants 174

1. DUTY CALLS

She held up the two bras in front of the mirror. The yellow one looked *nice*. Maybe she could find a pair of matching panties and play banana for a lucky someone to peel later tonight...

An alert suddenly came in on her work phone. Crime in progress within five hundred feet of her location. The system requested that she respond immediately and begin pursuit.

Detective Ashley Westgard of the Jacksonville Police Corps reluctantly hung the bras back on the rack. Her potassium fantasy would have to wait.

She checked herself in the mirror. The dark teal combat bra with sparkling glitter she'd been wearing for work lately looked damn good. She wasn't crazy about the ivory hoodie though—light gray seemed to accentuate her golden-tanned skin better.

Ash zipped the sweatshirt closed and marched out of the boutique clothing shop. She'd splurged here before and would definitely be back—but duty called, even when she was supposed to be done for the day.

She set her phone to start routing the new data to her matching silver video-bracelet and earring-speaker combo. An automated voice provided the latest information—Caucasian male, late twenties, suspected theft from one of the mall's high-end department stores.

Ash stuck the phone into her back pocket and began sprinting down the corridor, desperate to beat the in-house robot cops to the punch. She thought it was important to deliver *a personal touch* when apprehending lowlifes.

A piece of good news came in while she hurtled down an escalator: whatever the perp had stolen was manufactured with Sekür microchips, which were now broadcasting their location in real time. It would not be long before Ash and the shoplifter came face to face.

The voice in her ear now said that the embedded beacons had stopped moving somewhere in the vicinity of the cuisine court.

Ash slowed to a brisk walk. She was essentially wearing street clothes, so it was unlikely this perp would take her for a cop—sculpted shoulders and thighs notwithstanding. But this was Florida, lots of people were in great shape.

She turned a corner and entered a large open seating area. Dolls in skirts everywhere. Sitting by themselves drinking coffee. Half the chairs around them were occupied by fancy shopping bags overflowing with crepe paper.

Not many men in here. Typical of any shopping mall, really. She saw one dandy in a crushed velvet suit standing in line at the teriyaki booth empty-handed. Another was sitting at a large table snapping pictures of himself surrounded by his many purchases—Ash decided he was too conspicuous to be the thief.

Suddenly she darted down the center aisle heading for the restrooms. On the way she passed two other flamboyant men who were gesturing wildly to each other, but again trusted her intuition that neither was her prey.

She kicked open the gray steel door, then stomped her boot loudly. There he was. Hunched over the counter desperately clawing in search of the sewn-in microchips.

"Too late, you son of a bitch," Ash said. She heard the door close behind her. "So whatcha doin'?"

The man raised his arms pleading innocence. "Whaddya mean? I bought some presents for my girl, that's all."

"We'll see about that."

Ash sauntered up to the counter. She let her fingers run through the hard leather straps of the two designer handbags.

"Nice," she said. "Imported?"

"Yeah, probably." The man giggled nervously. "You wanna know what store, maybe get one for yourself?"

Ash shook her head. "No. I want to see your proof of purchase."

"My... proof?"

The man made a move toward the inside of his jacket. Ash leaped forward and pinned him back against one of the air dryers.

"And what's in *here?*" she snarled. "Something above-board or... ooh, something sharp!"

She pulled a folding knife out of his pocket, inspecting the contours of the maroon handle before whipping the blade open and pressing it against his cheek.

"This doesn't look like a receipt, now does it?"

"It's not what you think," the man gasped. "I just needed..."

Ash felt the tension in his body release as he crumpled

down onto the floor. She took a step back, but kept the knife at the ready.

"What is this shit?" she muttered. "What kind of a crook are you? Crying like a baby over purses, for Nano's sake!"

The man was now wiping tears out of his eyes. "You don't understand," he whelped. "I have to get these things for her, or else."

Ash glanced back at the loot, saying, "They look real posh, I'll give you that. But why are you *stealing?* I'm sure you get a stipend just like everybody else. These shouldn't be out of reach for you, if you save up."

The man sniffled. "This girl I been seeing, she got needs. *And,* she let me know I got competition. So I gotta keep up, 'cause she don't care if I run out of money."

"Competition, huh?" Ash said. "Like who?"

"Aw, shit... She told me, and I quote, 'all options are on the table.' That means other dudes, girls, hired help, plastic pickles, whatever."

"Sounds like my kind of lady."

"Yeah, yeah. You make it sound like it's all that. Always being chased. But maybe it's *you* looking over your shoulder worse than me! Think about that."

"Alright, you worm. Stand up, will ya?" Ash waved the knife encouragingly as he got back onto his feet. "Now what's the deal here? You tryin' to make a point?"

The man nodded at the purses. "Hey, what's gonna happen about that stuff?"

"We'll get to those gorgeous pieces of contraband soon, don't you worry. But, Mister Philosopher, it sounded like you were ready to share some *profound* insights about love. I'm all ears."

"Okay, uh..." He shrugged. "Feed me, fuck me, and I'm happy. Get it? I don't need VR or pills or gifts to get *me* off! But this girl... She's just like all the rest. My body ain't enough. Not my words... not the dinners... Hell, even these bags won't be enough!"

Ash said, "Then why are ya doing this, guy? Putting your freedom on the line for one little attention whore? You sound like a fool."

The man started tearing at his hair. "Because she's got me... She's my whole life! I *need* her!"

For just an instant, Ash felt a touch of compassion for this man. Somehow he had stumbled behind the curtain and gotten an unvarnished glimpse at the dating game's inner rules. But instead of using that wisdom to master the field, he had reverted back to infancy. Sneaking around, ripping off stores at an upscale shopping mall— and then bawling for sympathy after getting caught. It was unforgivable.

"No wonder she's looking anywhere and everywhere else," Ash said with disgust. "No way a sniveling piece of shit like you could keep her satisfied."

She closed the knife and put it into her hoodie pocket. Without warning, she lunged forward and cracked the man on his left jaw. He staggered away from the punch and slammed against a stall door. Feebly he held out his wrists.

"Cuff me, baby. It's okay. I couldn't face her now anyway."

"God, you're pathetic," Ash said. "But I don't have any handcuffs on me, because *I too* was doing a little shopping just now. So we're gonna march outta here on the honor system—and if you try to run, I'll have my foot up your ass in five seconds."

The thief bowed his head and dutifully shuffled toward the exit. Ash slung a purse under each forearm, giving herself a quick glance in the mirror before following him out.

This striped one is cute. *Pity I can't keep it.*

There were two rolling security bots waiting outside the restroom door. Ash handed the suspect and stolen merchandise off to them without a word, then strutted away.

It was Friday night and she was ready to party.

2. GIRLS' NIGHT OUT

"Yay, girls' night out!"

Steph, one of Ash's best friends, was lounging across a long seat in the back of their limousine. She raised her flute of champagne.

Ash and Kayla were seated across from her and clinked each other's glasses. Just then the limo swung a wide left turn onto a brightly lit street of shops that was packed with cars.

"Oh yeah," Kayla said. "The boulevard is *jumping* tonight."

Ash licked her lips. "Gonna be some flesh on parade, mm-hmm. Suck those guts in, girls. I don't want to hear anyone say these dresses make us look fat. 'Cause I am *off* the clock tonight."

"More like, on the cock," Steph said. She chomped her teeth.

"Hahaha," Kayla screamed with delight. She added, "But this is a no-bro zone, lady. You want any of that... we better turn this car around right now."

"Well, the night is still young."

"And so are we!" Ash declared. "Now let's get crawling!"

The driverless limousine sensed an opening and eased in close to the curb. As the doors unlocked and the trio spilled out onto the sidewalk, they heard a friendly female voice behind them say, "Thank you for choosing Queen Chariots. We're on call twenty-four..."

The street was alive. Women of all shapes and sizes wearing flashy outfits strutted in groups past the restaurants and shops. Luxury cars and SUVs with flashing neon trim eased down the clogged lanes in spurts. A motorcycle whizzed by, and heads turned as the passenger's skirt fluttered in the breeze.

Ash and her friends checked themselves in the reflection coming off the limo's window, then joined arms and sauntered away.

"Well," Kayla said, "what should we do first? Another drink? Eat? Or what?"

Steph said, "I'm tight. Let's go stretch."

They entered the reception area of a yoga studio.

"Welcome, ladies," the woman at the front desk said. "How are we tonight?"

"Ready for a good time," Ash said.

"Lovely. Did you just drop in for a quick fix or will you be joining us for a full session?"

"All we need's a stretch," Steph said.

"Certainly," the hostess replied. "If you'll please swipe your cards... Great. You have the floor."

Ash, Steph, and Kayla ran down the hallway and turned right into a room that had lavender walls in the breaks between floor-to-ceiling mirrors. Nearly a dozen other women were in various poses on floor mats.

The girls removed their high heels and placed them into cubbyholes, then skipped to an empty corner of the studio. They eased out of their fancy clothes and tossed them into a pile. Underneath they wore identical royal blue spandex bras and shorts.

"Aw, we look so cute!" Ash said.

"So, Steph," Kayla said, as she tilted her body to the side, "you got any updates for us on the Colombia trip?"

Steph sighed and sat down. "Yes, and no. The problem is," she said while leaning forward to grab her toes, "they keep finding ruins every place they want to build. Can't put a day spa next to some old temple used for human sacrifice, right?"

"Slay spa," Ash grunted. She had an arm pulled across her chest and was admiring her own eyes and glittery cheeks in the mirror. "I'd go."

"It's not that simple, you beast," Steph added as she sat back up. "Because, as the travel rep told me *most apologetically*, the UN has very strict rules whenever someone wants to break new ground. They gotta respect the native cultures, dead or alive."

"No wonder it's all taking so damn long. I've been hearing about this great new world almost my whole life. Sure would be nice to see it sometime."

"Oh, shush. There's plenty out there already. Including our own not-so-little-anymore city, thank you very much."

"Yeah, yeah. They jacked up Jacksonville, so what?"

"Just sayin'."

Kayla wiggled her shoulders. "So what's our backup plan? I don't *have* to go somewhere brand new."

"Are you serious?" Ash said, looking at Kayla in the mirror. "Being one of the first is half the fun. Who cares about seeing the Eiffel Tower or Machu Picchu anymore? I wanna drink piña coladas before shooting down the Mount Rushmore water slide!"

"Ooh, that must be so much fun!" Kayla began to sing, "We'll be drinkin', and no more Abe Lincoln..."

"Speaking of which," Steph said, popping to her feet. "I think I'm ready here. Let's liquor up."

The trio dabbed their faces with tissues, then put their party clothes back on. They slipped into their heels and bounded back into the night. A car that was crawling along beside them tooted its horn as the passenger gave a wave. Steph wagged her finger playfully before she followed Ash and Kayla into a bar.

Inside, all eyes were on a petite girl with pale skin and flowing black hair who was singing her heart out on the karaoke stage. Ash could see her nipples poking out through a ribbed white tank top.

A round of tequila shots arrived. Ash clinked her glass, then licked the salt between her thumb and forefinger slowly and lovingly as she stared at the singer. Finally she sent the drink down and bit angrily into the lime with a wild shake of her head.

The song ended and Ash leaned forward against the bar. She looked over her right shoulder, watching the girl leave the stage and slip down the narrow bar while everyone cheered. Just as the girl was about to pass behind, Ash scooted back and nudged hard against her hip.

Instantly another woman, who was much bigger and wore the same tank top with less flattering results, growled, "Hey, watch where you're going!"

Ash stood up to her full height. She looked into the singer's pretty eyes as she said, "Maybe *you* should watch where you're coming."

The big girl pawed her date to safety behind her, then said, "You want some of this, Blondie?"

"Not particularly. I want some of *that*."

Ash and the brute came nose to nose. The other patrons eased away in anticipation of a brawl. A hand with long red fingernails slid down between them.

"Come on, y'all," Kayla said soothingly. "It's too early for this kind of stuff. I don't want to visit the ER just yet, please."

As the two rivals separated, Ash said, "Just remember, bitches get stitches."

The other woman laughed disdainfully. "That's some big talk from a little labia."

"Which *you'll* never lick..."

"Okay, that's enough," Steph said, joining Kayla as they steered Ash out of the bar.

"Damn, Ash," Kayla marveled. "You brought the fire with you tonight!"

Ash chuckled. "That one was cute, though."

"Yeah, I know. But there's plenty of eye candy out here. Anyway, you need to cool off. Let's go lift weights."

The group dashed across the street and headed into one of several gyms that were on the boulevard. They checked in, stripped down again in the locker room, then stepped out onto the weight room floor wearing rental sneakers.

They spent half an hour doing deadlifts, pulldowns, and flipping tires. Steph passed most of the time flirting with one of the trainers, who had a large snake tattoo wrapped around the length of her left arm. It took all of Kayla and Ash's combined efforts to drag her away with only an exchange of contact information.

They hit another bar, this time without incident, then let loose for an hour at a packed dance club. Their next stop was a salon for quick touch-ups after all that sweating and grinding, before moving on to the phototorium. Here they booked a bright blue room filled with giant plush rabbits and a field of plastic tulips, then struck dozens of wacky poses as the cameras flashed. Afterward, they picked out their favorite shots to be delivered on their home printers.

It was after midnight now. Back on the sidewalk, Ash and her friends looked at each other.

"Well," Kayla said. "What should we do next?"

Steph tapped her chin. "Hmm... More drinks... more dancing... or maybe... *dicks?*"

They all laughed. Ash spanked Steph's ass.

"I don't know if I have the energy to get *involved* tonight," Kayla said. "If ya know what I mean."

"Whatever," Ash said. "How about some food?"

"Nah, I'm not hungry."

"Massages, anyone?" Steph proposed.

"Yeah!" Kayla said.

Ash raised an eyebrow. "Human or plastic?"

Kayla and Steph exchanged glances, then giggled.

"We better go bot," Steph said. "I have to do some work later in the morning. Coupla wandering digits and I'll be too wired to fall asleep."

Kayla smirked as she marched two fingers down Steph's belly. Solemnly she said, "Lead us not into titillation..."

Ash threw her arms over their shoulders and slurred, "Come on, you drunk skanks. Time to cut these engines before we get into real trouble."

"You're one to talk," Kayla scoffed. "Miss Dislocated Finger."

"And it was totally worth it. Knocked that lying bitch right out, remember?"

"What I remember is you trying to seduce the ambulance driver afterward."

"Hmm... Was that a guy or a girl?"

"Ladies, please!" Steph said. "We are *here*. It is time... to relax."

Ash held the massage parlor door open as her friends stumbled inside. Another wild night on the boulevard was coming to an end.

3. A NEW MALAISE

Saturday morning. *Late* morning. Ash was still in bed. Naked and feeling very relaxed.

That synthetic masseuse had worked wonders. The kneaders pushing down into her back like a big cat's paws. Ample pours of jasmine-scented gel rubbed with patient care into every inch of her long, slender body while soothing music filled the air.

She and her girls had floated out of the night spa into the SUV taxi they'd ordered, then leaned against each other drowsily before being dropped off at their apartments one by one.

But now Ash would have to get moving. Allow the dreams to evaporate as she amped herself back up for work. Detectives were still very much cops and the brass expected them to get their hands dirty while out in the streets.

Because criminals didn't care what your rank was. They didn't even seem deterred by all the cameras and sensors that were everywhere. Not only was crime up, but Ash thought it was getting more brazen—as if in defiance of the new models of robot officers that had recently joined the force.

Ashley Westgard wouldn't say that she resented or despised lawbreakers the same way some cops did. She felt she understood them—and besides, she was no angel herself. Although that didn't stop her from taking pleasure in grinding their faces into the dirt and calling them trash. Because there was just a certain line she wouldn't cross that the criminal element didn't respect...

She had a working theory about what was going on, which she called the dilemma of the steam valve. On one hand, the world was being built up and maintained virtually on autopilot by an interconnected network of machines that could assemble and repair themselves. But people still had doubts and flaws and uncontrollable passions that needed some kind of release. That didn't always make for a rosy picture.

Which is why Ash loved a good throwdown after words went too far. Or working the hormones into a frenzy, then spiraling upward all night with someone new. And as was the case lately, plotting with cold calculation how to climb her way up the police ranks and enter into gilded society.

What she couldn't forgive was the likes of that shoplifter from yesterday. People who tried to cut the line, and *then* came up with excuses after they got caught. Ash pondered whether that attitude was also part of this symptom she was seeing on the streets. A desperate flaunting that seemed to be saying "look at me" more than "I want this thing."

Some strange pressure was weighing people down, and Ash wondered if she was the only one who even noticed. While this keenness of mind *had* helped accelerate her promotion from beat cop to detective, she still was a flesh-and-blood animal, and often found

herself unable to resist falling prey to her own worst vices.

And if working in law enforcement kept you mostly above reproach, then being a *female* officer in 2045 meant you were untouchable. Ash's superiors didn't care what she or anyone else did in their off hours, as long as they kept clearing cases and the streets were safe. Still, Ash couldn't help but feel that she was starting to slip...

Because something was definitely changing inside her, as well as society at large. The steam valve wasn't enough to balance her out, or maybe she was just pushing it to the point of breaking down. Five drinks too many one day. Late-night calls to the street tough who sold her information and tasties. Churning and burning through women like she was shucking corn for a community potluck.

And then there was her most shameful weakness, which had started to boil over from a rare guilty pleasure into something she craved and relied on. Those *men*. The hired guns with flexing buns. But even they were mostly ineffective now, despite on paper—between the sheets, between her thighs—performing flawlessly.

Ashley Westgard was being hounded by some mysterious need. An itch she couldn't scratch, a blind spot that wouldn't come into focus. Just as society itself seemed sluggish within the fog of a new malaise. A pinched nerve that was driving people so crazy, they were willing to commit foolish crimes in the picture-perfect world that was being built just for them.

Ash dragged herself out of the California King bed and into her bathroom's enormous shower spa. Jets and sprays and rain pours hydrated her skin from all directions as she stretched, scrubbed, and did push-ups to rid herself of the last sleepy cobwebs.

To rinse away the alcohol. To clean hands soiled by

anonymous groping on a darkened dance floor. And to forget visions of a young girl's swollen nipples reaching out to her from the confines of a flimsy tank top—breasts which Ash had not gotten to devour.

A hot shower to clear her mind—and her eyes—as she tried to understand the hairline fractures she saw running across life's immaculate veneer.

4. THE NIGHT IS FEMALE

The City of Jacksonville had the honor of hosting the 2045 Cheri Chat at its famed Elixir Hotel, located in the bustling downtown waterfront area. While the conference had been held in more famous cities over the past decade, event planners were proud to showcase this Florida metropolis which had grown so rapidly in recent years.

Renowned female leaders from all over the country, as well as a dozen international guests, descended upon the hotel's convention center for a weekend of speeches, workshops, and opportunities to mingle with some of the world's foremost thinkers and women of action.

The Cheri Chat roster included legendary figures like Donna Pearcey and Shubhra Kanetkar, as well as key representatives of the new vanguard. Trina Nettles of Dartmouth and Iceland's goodwill ambassador Húna Halldórsson were among these exciting young presenters.

Saturday night's keynote speaker was none other than the indefatigable Mallory Quentin. She had cemented her reputation while serving as one of the original Essential Planners, that multinational group of diplomats tasked with guiding humanity through its "bright dawn of the soul" after a series of scientific advancements in the mid-2020s.

Ms. Quentin stepped away from government work eight years ago, in order to join the Department of Political Science at the University of Illinois. During her tenure, she also served on numerous committees, gave frequent testimony to the United Nations, and wrote countless policy papers that influenced the next generation of leading female minds.

The following summary features the highlights of her Cheri Chat presentation.

"Ladies and womyn, you have my warmest gratitude for coming along on this special journey tonight. I am proud to say that because of you, the *present* is female!"

The thousand attendees rose and filled the auditorium with applause. Mallory Quentin waved to each section of the capacity crowd, then motioned for them to retake their seats.

"Now," she continued, "let's review some of the incredible statistics that show just how far we've all come in a remarkably brief period of time."

The speaker moved away from the lectern and leaned against the giant burgundy Cheri Chat sign that sat in the center of the stage. As she spoke, graphics and charts appeared on the two large elevated screens directly above.

"Female enrollment in all higher education now accounts for ninety percent of the total. Most of the *other* students are older men who never got a degree the first time, or they went back to study some obscure niche field. In theory we could probably disqualify such applicants, citing the likelihood of no practical use. Buuuut, since they won't be competing with any of *us*," Quentin added with a shake of her head, "why not let them vie for the distinction of being the last male college graduate in America?"

A few laughs and snickers arose from the audience.

"Now, on to the professions!" Mallory slowly walked to the side of the stage. "At first blush the numbers might seem a bit perplexing, but when you really dig into the data you get this—"

The onscreen chart showed several categories of employment information divided by both gender and age.

"Do you see it? True, only seventy-one percent of veterinarians are women, but when we sort by *age*, we find that nearly ninety percent of vets under forty are female. What this means is that all those old-timers holding on to their practices from a bygone era, *that* is what explains the seemingly odd reality. But try as they might, these patriarchal doctors are in fact retiring in greater numbers every year. It's only a matter of time before 'puss in lab coats' completely dominate the industry."

Someone meowed loudly from the back of the auditorium. The women all laughed and turned their heads, but the theater was too dark to make out who the joker was. Mallory Quentin nodded politely, then resumed.

"But the biggest accomplishment of all has nothing to do with college admissions or careers. Records indicate that last year, in addition to the half-million state-supervised male births, less than seventy thousand additional baby boys were born outside of these facilities.

"That is an eight-percent reduction from the previous year, and down fourteen percent compared to five years ago. Huntresses and priestesses, the process is working! All we need to do is patiently stick to the program as laid out two decades ago, after humanity first experienced that trifecta of breakthroughs which promised so much—if only we could find the right leaders to entrust with that awesome responsibility of guiding the ship.

"Of course, *we* all know what came to pass during that serendipitous convergence of revolutionary technology and social progress. So say it with me now, ladies. Robots and exowombs and hemp, oh my! Robots... and exowombs... and hemp, oh my!"

Quentin paused to let the chant make its way through the crowd several times. Then she said, "It's really something when you think about it. Last century, when feminists first boldly proclaimed that the future would be female, little could they have imagined just how thoroughly we, their loyal descendants, would heed that clarion call.

"But how could we not have acted as we did? The fulfilled dream of artificial intelligence gave the world a tremendous tool, one that had the potential to change everything. And we remembered what happened *the last time* there was a great leap forward—men brought us the horrors of the World Wars! We simply couldn't afford to leave the fate of a yearning planet in the hands of destructive masculine urges. I think not!

"Because the old way of doing business—*his* way— was simply unsustainable. Of putting innovation on the shelf to extract more profits. Of sending armies to attack and invade, rather than envoys to cooperate and exchange culture.

"The end of necessity was not the end of history, but in fact the beginning of our destiny. To purge the old paradigm in favor of something that, while new, was firmly rooted in our intuitive female wisdom—and which had tragically lain dormant in chains for eons. But today, our voices are silent no more!"

A buzz was growing as the crowd viscerally responded to this inspiring account.

Mallory Quentin shook her fist, then said, "We are the ones who saw how perpetual motion, as realized by the Worker-Factory-Mechanic, could be the vanguard of an equitable future. All that was needed was a raw material capable of matching AI's tireless pace. We found it in that bountiful gift that comes from our dear Mother Earth: industrial-grade hemp.

"And ever since that day, females have been the eyes and conscience steering its awesome power from pole to pole. Transforming our world from one of scarcity and debt, into a joyful place of abundance and hope. It is no wonder—and no accident of history—that the women's movement ascended to oversee such a great pivot. Because every day and in every way, our superior ideas are enacting profound reforms and achieving lasting results!

"So many lovely new cities around the world have been built with ultra-modern technology, using green materials, and fashioned in styles consistent with their native cultures. We rebuilt Iraq, Libya, and Syria—and are turning Africa into a wonderland.

"Thank you all so very much for what you have done, and are doing still, to bring about this new heaven on Earth. It has been my honor to speak to you here in the beautiful city of Jacksonville, which just so happens to be a modern-day construction success story in its own right. Now that my work is done, I'm going to make my way to the refreshment stand, should any of you wish to discuss my research further. Good night!"

As Mallory Quentin exited the stage, she turned and waved once again to the audience. The robust applause continued for some time after she had disappeared from view.

A short young woman with milky beige skin and a

flattish nose that pinched in at the nostrils timidly approached the bar. She looked up at the statuesque blond woman in navy slacks and ivory blouse who was facing away and chatting with several other people. While waiting for a break in the conversation, she adjusted and readjusted the nylon bag that was on her shoulder.

"Excuse me," the girl said finally. She swung one leg in front of the other, wiggling her toes in the thong sandal. "Ms. Quentin?"

The middle-aged woman turned to her and smiled graciously. "Yes, my dear? How may I help you?"

"Hi. My name is Irma Dizon. I'm a freshwoman at the University of Tampa."

"Isn't that wonderful? So nice to make your acquaintance! Were you at my speech?"

The girl smiled. "It's an honor to meet you too. Oh yes, I saw it."

"Marvelous!" Quentin said. "And? What did you think?"

"It was very empowering."

"Well, good! Because that *was* the point." The woman laughed and drained the last of her champagne.

Irma took a step closer and said, "And now I have so many questions to ask you! Such as—"

"But what is all this?" Mallory exclaimed. "You don't have anything to drink. What can I get you?"

The girl blushed. "I don't know, ma'am. I was just hoping we could discuss..."

"Come now. It's my treat. Whatever you'd like."

"Oh, okay." Irma slowly looked over the dozens of bottles of liquor that sat on lighted shelves behind the bar. She said, "What's that bright yellow one?"

"It's called Lemonatica, darling," Mallory said. "Want a shot? Or would you prefer a cocktail?"

"I don't think I can handle a shot."

Quentin hailed a slender bartender in a silky sleeveless turtleneck blouse whose long hair was coiled on top of her head like a pyramid.

"Hey, Rosie!" she called out. "My friend here needs a LemBomba. And another glass of bubbly for me. Charge it all to the room."

As the bartender was topping off the champagne, Mallory pointed to a table that had just freed up along the wall.

"Irma, quick! Go grab that for us!"

A few moments later, the two women were seated across from one another in a booth which had old-fashioned button tufts set into the dark brown leather.

"Cheers," Mallory said as she raised her drink. Irma dropped her shoulder bag onto the seat and clinked glasses. "So, young lady. What's on your mind?"

"Oh my goodness," the girl said. "I can't believe this is happening!" She began to rifle through her bag, then pulled out a small purple binder and turned to a tabbed page. "You write a lot about the great convergence. Like, the inventions, and the political changes that made it all possible..."

"Yes, that's correct. And?"

Irma sipped from her straw, then consulted her notes. "But I was hoping to hear more about the challenges you see on the horizon. Since things are always—"

"Mallory, dahhhhling!" a voice crooned from halfway across the bar. An enormously round individual decked out in the season's fashion craze—left side with hair cut short and wearing the clothes of a man, the right permed and sporting a feathery dress—came surging over to the booth. "And who may I ask is this adorable little nymph?"

"Good evening, Gaia," Mallory said with affected coolness. "Aren't you even going to make mention of my chat?"

"Pff," the rotund diva said. "The last thing you need is more ego stroking. But do tell me who your friend is."

"This is Irma, a quite remarkable student who—"

"What a pleasure! Now Irma, behold. I am Her Opulence Gaia Sauce, at your service."

Irma took Gaia's right hand into her own and they rubbed fingertips. She said, "This is all so nice! Tonight I never imagined that I would—"

"Shush!" Gaia implored. "High priestess or not, we all like to mingle. And *I* should very much like to learn more about you."

"Now, now, Sauce," Mallory interjected. "The fish tank in this restaurant is still quite full."

Gaia gave a hearty laugh. "So true. But Irma, tell us. Do you have a *boyfriend* right now?"

The girl's mouth fell open. She glanced back and forth between the two women. "I, uh..."

"Oh my!" The diva snapped her head to the side. "Is that... Yes, it is! Barretina has just arrived. Do excuse me, ladies, but I absolutely *must* move along now..."

Irma watched the massive Gaia glide with apparent ease through the packed bar. Glancing down at the tabletop, she saw that Mallory Quentin had taken hold of her hand.

"You know something?" the older woman said. "I think you have beautiful eyes."

"Oh... thank you." Irma looked up at the ceiling.

"Miss Irma. Did you *really* want to ask me about my professional opinions? Or was that just your icebreaker?"

"No, truly!" Dizon protested. "Ms. Quentin, I love learning about science... self-replicating machines... and all the great things just waiting to be discovered! I mean, we're already so blessed to live in a time when humanity is free from relying on brute male force..."

"Mm-hmm." Mallory had closed her eyes and was stroking the top of Irma's hand. "Tell me more."

Irma moved her hand away and flipped through her papers again. "And here," she said breathlessly, "when they perfected genetic design and the artificial uterus. Suddenly no more birth defects, mutations—and yay!—ending our curse of having to carry a child around for all those months."

Quentin leaned back in her seat. "So tell me, Irma. Does that mean you're a wombie?"

"Of course! Just look—do you see any flaws?"

Mallory slowly studied the girl's fingers, her eyes, her neck, and the curves along the front of her cashmere sweater. Irma felt a chill of excitement as goosebumps sprouted all over her arms.

"Filipina, aren't you?" Quentin said.

"Yes. How did you guess?"

"Maybe it's those adorable cheeks of yours." Mallory's eyes twinkled. "Oh science, how I love thee... But woe is *me*, for I am not nearly as perfect as your precious jewel Irma."

"Yes, well..." Irma's head wobbled. Her fingers danced on the edge of the table. "But, but... your work. What new stressors do you think might... Because... as a future leader myself... Maybe one day... Essential Planner too..."

"Aw," Mallory pouted, "why do you want to get into all that boring stuff in a crowded place like this? 'Cause you know, most people go to bars to loosen up." She tilted the champagne glass to her lips with a wink, then motioned at the yellow beverage.

Irma regained her composure and said, "It matters to me, I swear! I keep thinking about this editorial you wrote last year, 'Utopia is Not a Derogatory Term.' You said that we have to watch out for critics as much as for changing tides. I want to know more!"

Quentin sighed. "Here's the thing. It could take me *hours* to spell it all out for you. And the seats here are just so uncomfortable... Oh, but I know! One perk of being a guest speaker is that I have a whole suite to myself inside this very hotel! And it's fully stocked. We can eat, drink, take in the city views, and I'll tell you all about what I see in my crystal ball. Sound fair?"

"Hooray!" the girl gushed. "Ms. Quentin, when I got my ticket for this weekend, I never *dreamed* I would meet someone famous like you. In my classes we—"

Irma stopped abruptly. Mallory had brought a finger to her own lips and was staring at her.

"There's no need to explain anything, dear girl," Quentin said quietly. "Or to be nervous. We both have something the other wants."

Irma scrunched her shoulders in and looked away.

Mallory Quentin rose from the booth. She turned to Irma and extended her hand.

"Come," she said. "The night is female."

5. ECSTASY

"Irma, have you ever been to a Clam Bake?"

Mallory Quentin was lounging across one of the soft leather couches that sat in the middle of her high-ceilinged, wide open hotel suite. A hookah was on the floor beside her, and she slowly brought the orange mouthpiece to her lips. She blew smoke out in a high arc from right to left.

Irma Dizon was seated on the floor a few feet away, leaning back against a love seat. Her binder was open across her knees, and she held a rainbow-striped cigarette between her fingers.

"I've heard of them," Irma said, taking a puff. "But I never actually saw one."

"Then it's your lucky night," Mallory said. She reached for her bottle of Athena Ale that was on the glass coffee table, and drank the last sip before tossing it onto the shag rug underneath. "Nicer hotels like this usually carry them. Shall we take a look?"

"Um, sure. But Ms. Quentin, you still haven't given me any tips about what course corrections my generation might expect to oversee. Can you at least give me a hint?"

"All in good time, I promise you. But so much serious talk, my heavens!"

"I'm sorry."

"And do call me Mallory. Now truly, we *must* teach you how to relax."

Mallory swung off the couch and offered Irma her hand, pulling the petite younger woman up from the floor and then draping an arm around her shoulders. She leaned over slightly to pluck another bottle of beer off the high counter as they passed the kitchen and entered the bedroom suite.

The recessed blue floor lights that lined the walls were dimmed very low. An antique poster bed decorated with lace curtains occupied the right side of the room, and Irma absently ran her fingers through the soft fabric until her attention was drawn to a dark cocoon-like object near the far wall. It was the size of a deep float tank and its top edge curved up to over four feet from the ground.

Irma turned her head and looked quizzically into Mallory's eyes.

"Would you like to touch it?" Mallory whispered. Irma nodded. They approached and Mallory slid the girl's hand across the grooved surface of the synthetic black shell. "Feels like a real clam, doesn't it?"

"Oh yes," Irma said.

Mallory gazed at the girl's face, so soft and beautiful in the faint light. She leaned forward and placed her moistened lips upon Irma's mouth, letting her tongue loose to probe for resistance. She felt Irma's body go slack, but the lips puckered and began to engage in their own hesitant exploration.

Mallory pulled away and smiled. "Now," she said, "let us turn you into a pearl..."

She pressed a button on the underside of the shell and

they heard the top come loose. It rose slowly and a soft pink glow emanated onto the walls and ceiling. The women peered inside.

The lower half was sculpted and curved like a spa, and three-quarters filled with a gooey substance that bubbled gently. The underside of the clam top was crammed with dozens of dangling rubbery objects in different shapes, sizes, and textures. The mass jiggled slightly after the hydraulic opening motion stopped.

"Take off your clothes," Mallory said.

She helped unbutton Irma's linen blouse, taking a moment to kiss or caress each newly exposed area of skin. Irma shuddered when she heard a little zip and felt her skirt fall to the floor. Mallory giggled playfully.

"Just you wait," she said, placing Irma's hands onto her own breasts for a moment. "This'll have you twitching for a week!"

"What's going to happen?" the girl asked nervously as she slipped out of her bra and panties. "Are you getting in with me?"

"Sadly, no," Mallory said with a smile. "This is only the solo model. But I'll be waiting for you on the bed when you're through."

"Umm... Okay then."

"Now, let me help you up. There..."

Irma stepped onto the stool that was attached to the base of the unit. Mallory held one of her hands as she climbed over the edge and entered the warm, sloppy fluid. She eased onto her back and slid down into a tangled cluster of rubbery coral reef and gelatinous seaweed, pushing her legs through until finally settling as if she were in a normal bathtub.

Mallory winked at her and slowly closed the lid. Irma watched the assortment of squishy appendages descend all around her face and the tops of her knees. The shell clicked shut.

"Irma, can you hear me?" Mallory's voice came in through small speakers on either side of her head.

"Yes, Ms. Quentin."

"Good, good. I'm going to start the sequence in a minute. If for any reason you panic or need to get out, the inside door handle is connected to the plastic lip on your left side. Do you see the small printed label?"

"Yes, thank you," Irma said.

"Pull out and twist to stop the jets. Pull again and it'll pop right open. Now, my love, are you ready?"

"I think so."

"Then close your eyes. And prepare... for ecstasy..."

Irma heard a series of rumbles followed by a low hum, then watched as the jelly liquid began to churn like a simmering pot of pink soup. Dreamy electronic music faded in through the speakers. Lights flickered and sparkled throughout the capsule. And finally the suspended rubbery mass dipped below the surface and started to vibrate.

As the plastic nubs and soft spikes rhythmically meandered over the surface of her body, Irma involuntarily licked her lips. Then she felt larger, harder appendages move in and begin to probe her nether regions.

She moved a hand down the length of her body and brushed away a foam cylinder that was nudging up against her tuft of pubic hair. She began to stimulate herself, while her free hand absently swatted at anything that tried to access the area.

Her every curve and crevice was being stroked and sloshed as her mind danced in a budding avalanche of tingles. A stray noodle wandered into her mouth and she sucked on it tenderly, then gave a vicious chomp before pushing it aside.

Higher and higher Irma's head swirled until she lost all control of herself. Her useless hands floated away into the dense flora of this erotic swamp. Squishy tendrils and textured nubs burrowed their way into the void between her weakened, quivering legs. She was now at the mercy of this rapturous aquatic massage.

Suddenly her body exploded into a seizure of delirium. She bounced around like a hooked marlin while absorbing the thousand little fingers that had possession of her every nerve ending and pore. She moaned as she never had before. She gasped for air, or maybe it was reprieve, as her mind's eye now sensed with terrifying awareness the approaching headlight in the distance.

When she collided soul-first with that incomprehensible force and felt the existentially vaporizing orgasm-beyond-orgasm, she unleashed a primal scream that channeled all of the ancient goddesses who had once roamed the earth and ruled—before that devil, the patriarchy, constricted the magical fairy world into a repressive nightmare.

As her scorching inner fire slowly burned itself out, Irma Dizon sensed that the bubbles around her were subsiding. Through half-closed eyelids she could see that all of the tentacles were floating limp and dead on the surface of the bath. She exhaled deeply.

"Irma?" Mallory's gentle voice came to her through the speakers. "Are you okay?"

Irma blinked. "Yes," she whispered. "My goodness... Very much, yes!"

"Lovely! Give yourself a few minutes to cool down in there. When you're ready, I'll be out here with fresh drinks. But please, take your time."

"Thank you," Irma sighed. She was spent—but still, she could feel a little spark darting around her body. Something truly wonderful had awakened inside her, and it was powerful on a level that textbooks could never explain.

She knew that Mallory was outside waiting for her, and that this clam shell experience was only the beginning of their night together. The newfound strength would carry her through whatever other lessons her hero intended to share in the hours that followed. Irma hoped she could return the favor and bring Mallory pleasure as well.

But first, she just needed to rest for a few minutes before leaving this warm cocoon...

Irma opened her eyes. A dull pink light illuminated the pod. She tried to adjust her body, but her foot was caught in the foliage at the bottom of the tub. Now she realized that most of the liquid had drained out.

She reached left and grabbed the handle, then tugged on it as she had been instructed. The clam shell top released and slowly eased itself fully open.

She held onto the edge of the lip for balance, then lifted herself out of the slippery and scratchy undergrowth with one last squish of her feet. After stepping softly onto a large bathmat that was beside the step stool, Irma gave a shiver as she squinted into the darkened room.

"Mallory?" she said. Her voice was faint and scratchy.

After hearing no response, she looked more carefully around the suite. There was no one in the bed. To her right was a wooden chair with a bathrobe neatly folded on the seat. A note on top said, "Hey, sleepy head. Take a shower and rinse off. I'm making us some snacks. Luv, MQ."

Irma suddenly got self-conscious and traced a finger down the side of her body. She held it up in the beam cast by one of the floor lights. The tip was covered in a sticky goo. She grabbed the robe with her other hand and ran into the bathroom.

Two tea candles on either side of the sink were burning, and the flickering light was just enough for Irma to make her way around the elegant space. Plus, she didn't really want to know what her body looked like covered in this slimy stuff under bright lights.

Irma entered the clear glass shower and felt the residue peel away from her skin. She hesitated for a moment before grabbing the natural loofah, then smiled to herself and scrubbed the rest of her body clean.

She stepped out of the bathroom a few minutes later. The robe was tied loosely so that her breasts showed, and her wet black hair was twisted up in a cute topknot. Expecting to see Mallory lying nude across the bed, and perhaps sucking on a chocolate-covered strawberry, Irma put on a big smile...

But the room was still empty. She glanced inside the Clam Bake just to be sure, then opened the door and went out into the living room.

All was dark except for the glow of the city coming in through the windows. To her right, a small light was on above the kitchen sink. She saw a block of cheese sitting next to a plate of crackers, but still no sign of Mallory. She walked toward where they'd had drinks earlier, but stopped when she felt her feet step into a spill.

In the near-darkness, Irma's eyes widened as she leaned her weight forward to look more closely at the gap between the couch and the coffee table.

She screamed.

6. SCENE OF THE CRIME

A half dozen stone-faced female police officers in navy blue held the line against a crowd that was gathered outside the Elixir Hotel. Streetlight flashed off their silver badges whenever they took an imposing step to brush back nosy onlookers.

Three local news crews had set up away from the rabble near one of the hotel's front support columns. Each gorgeous reporter holding a foam-capped microphone was five foot seven, slender, and wearing high heels. One had pale white skin, another caramel, and the third dark chocolate.

Like a dance troupe that was waiting for their cue, these newswomen whipped their heads to the side in unison at the loud pop and rumble of a revved engine. The cameras also swung around in the direction of the noise after being prompted by the reporters' snapping fingers.

The crowd now stepped away from the police line and moved to the hotel driveway's entrance. They pushed in close and walked alongside an armored ATV which had an airbrushed design of white smoke plumes on the side plating.

Everyone fell back when the fearsome vehicle stopped and its grumbling motor went silent. Toned bare arms rose up and placed fingerless leather gloves upon a sparkling charcoal helmet. The letter *A* was emblazoned in red on each side.

As the helmet slid up, bystanders first saw the hard but elegant curve of the rider's jaw, then beheld a sensuous mouth glistening with lip gloss. Next came the thin nose which angled down in a perfectly straight line. The crowd's gaze continued further upward as the helmet finally came off. Two rope-thick blond braids cascaded down at the sides. It was as if a milkmaid had been cast to play a hard-rock music video vixen.

The rider brought the helmet down to her hip and cradled it like a basketball, then turned to the onlookers and opened her scintillating blue eyes. She gave a confident smirk, nodding to the crowd with her whole upper body.

"Ash, Ash!" someone yelled. A girl of ten or twelve ran up to the side of the ATV. "Can I have your autograph?"

The woman gave a devilish smile, lips curving up at the sides as perfectly straight and shimmering white teeth came into view. "Hold this," she said, then handed the helmet to the young fan.

A leg that began nearly as thick as livestock but tapered down beautifully like a ballerina's, now swung over the seat as she dismounted from the vehicle. The crowd again instinctively moved back, some out of respectful fear, but others in lusty awe of the prime specimen on full display before them.

She was a five-foot-nine hybrid of Swedish supermodel and ripped gym rat, wearing a sparkling teal combat bra that barely contained breasts large enough to dazzle, but not too cumbersome to get in the way of workouts or a fist fight.

Thighs carved into stone by squats and deadlifts rippled under skintight faint-gray pants that were equally equipped for tackle football or hot yoga. There was a hint of visible skin below—just as tan as the exposed midriff and lusciously freckled arms—and a silver charm bracelet was wrapped around the right ankle. Tufts of Husky-colored fleece protruded from the tops of eight-eyed black leather boots to complete the outfit.

The young fan looked up at this force of nature desperately. "Please?" she said.

"Okay. If you insist."

"I do!" The girl reached into her jacket pocket, but stopped rummaging when a finger bright with glittery nail polish was pointed directly at her eye.

The Amazon drew this finger back and placed it into her own mouth, removing it slowly with a 'pop' when she released the tip. The finger was then pressed against the girl's forehead, gliding and swirling across the surface before falling away.

"There," the rider said in a sweet and dainty voice. "Ash."

The girl tapped two fingertips against her wet forehead. Then she, along with the entire crowd, turned to watch as Ash pulled on a zip hoodie and bounded past the police line.

Her head-exploding buttocks rippled and flexed triumphantly with each step she took toward the hotel entrance.

The glass sliding doors opened and Detective Ashley Westgard took stock of the scene in the lobby. Cops with hands on hips talking to paramedics whose arms were folded. Confused guests sitting with their bags while hotel staff scurried back and forth.

And there, with the faulty titanium replacement leg, was her sometime partner Detective Theodore Gillard talking on the phone. While she waited for him to finish, Ash reached into her bra and pulled out a piece of hard candy. The discarded plastic wrapper had barely hit the lobby floor before a tiny bot zipped over and snatched it up.

When the melon-flavored sucker was halfway gone, Ash saw Gillard lean onto his cane and nod at her. She tucked the sweet back into her bra and approached.

"Well?" she said.

The pallid man put his phone away and hobbled closer to her.

"Howdy, partner," he said. "So glad you could join us on such short notice. Saturday night and all, I thought surely you..."

"No, I was free," Ash said, her mind flashing back to the basement brothel she'd been forced to leave well before getting any kind of satisfaction. Maybe it was for the best—otherwise she might be a scatterbrained mess rushing to a crime scene without any time to pull herself together. Reputation still mattered, in some ways at least.

"Well, good," the man said. "A nasty SOB just gave you something to do."

"Don't get my hopes up. You know how much I hate boring crimes."

"Not this one. Which is probably why Chief wanted you in on it. Shall we?"

Gillard struggled forward slowly. Ash kept pace, looking around the lobby once more. When they entered the elevator, he said, "Push twenty."

"Mmm, the penthouse. I can already feel my pheromones rising."

"And if I was even half the man I used to be..."

"Then you'd end up as part of the next pair of boots I'm having made."

Gillard eyed Ash's cleavage. It protruded brazenly from inside her barely zipped hoodie. He said, "I hope when I'm finally put out to pasture, that you'll remember me for other things."

Ash folded her arms. "Some men would consider it an honor to donate a pound of flesh to my shoe collection."

"Young brutes who have nothing bigger than themselves to live for, no doubt. They need *God*, not *goddesses*."

"Who cares what men want? Or even think?" She shook her head and pretended to spit.

Ash stomped out loudly when the elevator doors opened. She didn't wait for Ted. He proceeded slowly after her and called out, "I'm so sorry there wasn't a staircase for you to run up in a huff to complete the scene."

Ash threw out her left arm and flipped him the bird.

"Very impressive," he said more loudly as the distance between them increased. "But you don't even know where you're going!"

Ash stopped and turned her head. "Out with it. What room?"

"2011. But can you please—"

Ash moved down the hallway quickly and turned left at a split after reading a small sign on the wall indicating the room numbers. She soon came upon two female cops who were posted outside one of the doors. She recognized them from an informal police social club she had attended a few times—good whiskey, honest card games, no gossip allowed. The officers nodded at her as she entered the suite.

Ash immediately sensed that this might be her first

good case in months. Which would provide the motivation necessary to actually focus on her job. Instead of hemorrhaging money buying accessories for the ATV. Or on manicures, followed by clothing purchases to match the new shade her nails had been painted. Although the prospect of missing an appointment with Zuze at the salon *was* annoying, sometimes you had to make sacrifices in the pursuit of real glory...

She felt a squeeze at the side of her tummy.

"Excuse me, Detective Blubber!"

Ash turned and stared daggers at Detective Gillard. He had dropped down in the door jamb and was out of breath.

She sighed, tapping at the little area of belly fat with her fingers before offering the man a hand up. He had covered for her a number of times since her promotion nearly two years ago, so she could only despise him so far. He was an aging man from the old world whose days of relevance and effectiveness were dwindling.

"Thanks," Gillard said. "You're a real public servant. Ready to work now?"

"Game on," she replied.

"White female. Forty-four. Slashed throat. Come take a look."

They entered the spacious suite. It had an austere design with limited art on the walls, and dark floor-length drapes hung at intervals along the windows and sliding door that filled the entire left side. The flooring consisted of large, hand-grooved concrete that was brightened by several area rugs.

The leather couches and an end love seat formed a U shape around a coffee table that sat on a shag throw—and wedged between them was the body of a woman in a silky floral kimono laying on its side. Two paramedics and another officer stood silently by the windows.

Ash quickly surveyed the remainder of the space. Three pools of blood connected by a line of spatters—as well as a number of messy bare footprints—ran along the floor from the body to the small kitchen. A room service cart stood nearby, with a covered plate and silver ice bucket atop the white linen—the champagne bottle inside was unopened. A lamp and side table at one end of the couch had been overturned. Shards of ceramic had skittered off toward the dining area that was tucked on the other side of the kitchen wall.

"What do we think happened?" she asked. "Robbery gone bad?"

"Nothing appears to be missing," Detective Gillard said. "But the vic *was* here for a weekend conference, not a vacation, so we don't think she would have brought much in the way of valuables. They didn't take whatever jewelry she had on, at least."

"Mm-hmm. Got an ID on her yet?"

Ash walked over to the windows and gazed out on the skyline of high-rises and twinkling lights of boats floating on the water.

Gillard pulled a tablet out from inside his police-issue jacket. He tapped around the screen for a moment before holding out a forearm. Ash heard a subtle hum and turned toward him, then took hold of the piece of paper that came curling out of his sleeve.

"Mallory Quentin," she heard him say as she reviewed the information on this up-to-the-second printout. "Highly respected social scientist and policy maker. Not one for the kind of gruesome death we have here, I should think."

"No," Ash said. She stepped back and pivoted on one of her boot heels to face the room. "You said she was at a conference. What kind of event are we talking about?"

"This year's Cheri Chat is being held in the hotel's

convention center. I'm sure you've heard of it before. One of those 'girls rock' pep rallies we can't seem to get enough of. Ms. Quentin gave a presentation earlier this evening."

"Yeah? What did she have to say? Anything controversial enough to piss someone off? Maybe they tracked her down and killed her."

"Not likely," Ted said. "Just the usual rah-rah speech. There'll probably be fifty just like it this weekend."

"Chin up, Detective," Ash said playfully. "It isn't Female Appreciation Month yet! Think of all those mandatory seminars you'll get to attend, and—"

Ash froze. She took a step toward the love seat and bent down. She turned her head back to Gillard.

"There's two glasses here," she said.

"Bingo!"

"That means Miss Mallory had company. *Welcome* company. Lover's quarrel? Or a tryst gone horribly wrong?"

The man smiled. "Almost, my dear little Miss Westgard. Try, *one-night-standus interruptus*."

"So a *third* person was involved? How can you be so sure?"

"Follow me," Ted said, waving his hand toward the door. "I'd like you to meet the next-to-last person to see Mallory Quentin alive."

Detective Gillard's artificial knee squeaked and clicked as he made his way across the suite toward the exit. Ash paused to apply fresh lip gloss before following him out.

They turned a corner in the hall and came face to face with two other police officers. One was a man, older than fifty but still in top physical condition. Ash flexed her arms and shoulders, shaking her head at him as she and Ted entered this second hotel suite. It was almost pitch black inside except for the light coming in through the windows.

"Hello?" Ted called out gingerly.

"We're over here, at the dining table," a female voice responded softly. "But please don't turn on the lights."

Gillard took a step forward and Ash heard a weird click. His leg had locked up. He turned to her plaintively and held out his arm. "Do you mind?"

She ducked her shoulder under his, but then didn't make a move. Suddenly she bent her knees and scooped him up into her arms to carry him across the room.

"I don't know whether to be humiliated or flattered," he said wryly. "You've swept me off my feet!"

"Foot," Ash clucked. "Good thing for the sake of your pride it's so damn dark in here."

"Knowing you, something tells me you may never have done this before. With a man at least. What'll the boys think when I tell 'em I popped your threshold cherry?" he added in a whisper.

"I wonder what else might go pop if I tossed you down right now?" Ash stopped walking and looked Ted in the eyes.

"You'd never do it," he said. "*Even though* I'm a man, you know how much of myself I gave to the force. The thin blue line, remember? You carry that same badge— hidden *somewhere* in that whore's getup they let you wear as a uniform."

"Why are you so sure you know what made me want to become a cop? Don't make assumptions about *who* I protect and serve."

"Hmph," Gillard muttered. "Point taken. Thanks for the ride, but I think our little honeymoon is over. And I do hope you'll find some of that 'why I serve' motivation when you meet our witness here."

Ash exhaled, hoping to release the rush of tension that

had suddenly come over her. She set Ted down and hated herself for doing it so gently. But he *was* a good cop...

Over in the far corner of the suite, a small rectangle of light emitted from a tablet on the dining table. Ash and Gillard drew near. A prim brunette in a pantsuit sat comforting someone in a bathrobe whose head was bowed over praying hands.

The woman looked up at them. "Hello, Ted. I see you've brought... *her*."

"What can I say? Chief knows she's one of the best." Gillard patted Ash on the shoulder. "I'll leave you to it. Don't let me down."

Ash watched the frail man disappear into the darkness. Then she pulled out a chair and sat down.

"Howdy," she said.

The robed figure lifted her head. Deep dark pupils looked up fearfully. A strand of black hair fell across the face and was brushed away. Ash felt a selfish wave of power thinking about how easily she could pick up this dainty girl with one arm and drag her off to be a personal slave...

But this was not the true emotion. Ash was a local star, a goddess on wheels who could have any little tart she wanted. Inexplicably, the brothel from earlier tonight now came to mind. She'd been going there more often lately. Too often. Some nights running through more than one male trick trying to reach that place which had become so elusive.

Women had once been able to take her there easily. But maybe, Ash now wondered, it was the *process* and not the ending that was the key. Experiencing real live human cock, and not the substitute of little hands squirming inside, or even the most anatomically correct pulsing dildos that could be had in any color, texture, and size.

It was the strong gripping arms, the forceful mouth, the musky smell—all of it driven by the synapses firing within the mind of a biological male. Something that no computer or factory could mimic well enough to fool Ash's deepest receptors. Like the timbre of a human voice whispering filthy promises in her ear, or feeling the raw surge of delicious terror when a muscular man threatened to *obliterate* her.

Even the ones who were half her size had a way of taking charge that, upon later reflection, both infuriated her and drenched her panties. They handled her not just muscle for muscle, but inevitably melted her down into a powerless puddle. It was to their credit—although more likely because of their low legal status than from any sense of honor—that these male prostitutes were tender and forgiving in her weakest moments. They never kissed and told.

And now Ash was staring into the eyes of a scared little woman who needed her help, not her lustful gaze. She zipped her hoodie up to the collar, somehow hoping that in covering herself she would stop feeling so horny in the middle of a murder investigation. That exhibitionist trick always worked wonders when interrogating male suspects—they got sloppy and couldn't keep their stories straight when staring at her tits—but there was no place for that kind of display tonight.

This girl was a *victim*, not a perp. It was time to get serious. Maybe later she could see about purchasing a nano boost from one of the street hustlers under her protection. A few good chemically enhanced masturbation sessions and she might be able to wean herself off this brothel habit, which was costing her more than just financially.

"Okay, Kathleen," Ash said to her colleague, "what am I looking at?"

"*Who* you are looking at," Kathleen said as she straightened her papers, "is Irma Dizon. She's eighteen, and currently enrolled at the University of Tampa. She's here in town for the weekend Cheri Chat. Irma happened to cross paths with Ms. Quentin, and later accompanied that woman up to her suite."

"And then what?"

"I think Irma had better fill you in on the details. Can you do that, hon?" Kathleen rubbed the girl's back gently.

Irma wiped her eyes. "Okay. I'm tired, but I'll try."

Ash said to her, "Had you ever met Ms. Quentin before?"

"No. I mean, I'm a really big fan of her ideas. So I've posted comments on her site before. But a lot of people do that. After the talk I just wanted to say hi and thank her for all her work, because it inspired me to pursue my degree. But then she bought me a drink and wanted to hang out."

"So, she tried to seduce you, basically?"

"I... I don't know."

"Come on!" Ash scoffed. "She took you back to her room, right? What did you all get up to in there—surely not crafting policy?"

"Watch your tone," Kathleen snapped. "Irma is virtually witness to a murder, and here you are badgering her with faux-moral outrage. Of all people, Detective Westgard. *You?!*"

Ash sat back in her chair coolly. "What do you mean by, 'virtually'?"

"Well, Irma was not only not in the living room at the time of Ms. Quentin's killing, she may actually have slept through it. For up to an hour, in fact."

"Look, I saw that crime scene. Whatever happened in there was *brutal*. How in the hell could anyone not wake up during something so awful?"

"Ashley," Kathleen said, "I assume you're a woman of the world. Are you by any chance familiar with the pleasures of a product known as the Clam Bake?"

Ash sat still for a moment. She chuckled, which quickly grew to a sarcastic laugh. "Are you telling me that while Mallory Quentin was being slaughtered, Irma here was out cold inside a Clam Bake shell? No goddamn way!"

"I've heard they're quite relaxing."

"Kathleen, *a massage* is relaxing. I can't imagine that I'd be taking a cat nap after sloshing around in all that plastic spaghetti."

"But it's true," Irma whispered. "I've never felt *anything* like that before. Our sex ed teacher back in high school, she knew how to do a lot—but this tonight was... overwhelming."

Ash raised her eyebrows, then waved her hand with a shake of the head. "Okay, let's assume this clam thing did all you said it can do. Then what? You wake up, go look for Mallory—because now it's *her* turn for some fun after you've been all buttered up—and?"

"I took a shower first to get all that stuff off me, then I went to the living room. *I stepped in her blood!*"

Irma's face crumbled and she fell forward onto the tabletop in tears.

"How did it go from that," Ash said to Kathleen, "to us finding out?"

"This brave girl," Kathleen replied, "despite her terror, had the wherewithal to find the phone and call for help. But Ashley, I think she's too worked up right now to say any more. Let me take her down to the station for some rest, and then later you or someone else can talk to her after the shock has worn off."

Ash looked at the weeping girl. Her body was heaving under the bathrobe.

"Fair enough," she said. "Get her on out of here. I'm gonna stick around and jot down some notes. You have any idea who this third party might be?"

"I'm a psychologist," Kathleen said, "not a detective. I help the living. You... crawl around in the gutter trying to figure out why they turn up dead."

"Just be sure you keep this one alive. She may know more than she realizes."

"I understand. Now Irma," Kathleen said as she stood up, "can you be a good girl and come downstairs with me?"

Ash watched Kathleen lead Irma to the door. After it had clicked shut, she unzipped a pocket on the side of her thigh and pulled out a flexible rectangular sliver. She kicked a boot up onto the chair Irma had been sitting in, then began writing out her first reactions to the case with her fingernail.

She looked over at the couches which were barely visible in the dim light—the layout here was almost identical to the suite where the murder had taken place. Ash's eyes wandered in the direction of the bedroom. She stowed the tiny notepad back inside her pocket and walked to the door. It was cracked. Slowly she pushed it open, then flicked the dimmer switch up a notch.

There it was. This suite was also furnished with a Clam Bake. High-end PleasureQuarium model with deep mahogany finish. In one breathless motion Ash began stripping off her clothes—hoodie yanked open and dropped inside out, combat bra lifted up and helicoptered away, boot laces clawed desperately apart, stretchy pants fought down and stomped off, and—there was no g-string. Because she'd forgotten it in her rush to leave the brothel on this work emergency. *Or* one of those bastards swiped it for his own collection...

Ash shrugged her shoulders. It didn't matter now.

None of it did. Not those strutting concubines. Not her police partner who gave too much lip for someone on the way out. Not that by-the-book bitch Kathleen. Not even whimpering little Irma Dizon.

Because right now she, Ashley Westgard, was about to test the waters of a Clam Bake for the very first time. And maybe everything people said about it was true. Maybe she too would soar beyond ego and jealousy and cravenness, and finally transcend pleasure itself in an explosion that reset the circuit breaker of her soul.

Ash dipped her foot into the glowing pink goo. She eased her bronzed body down through the squishy and scratchy tangles below the surface. After pulling the top down and closing herself in, she leaned back against the foam head support. She put the half-eaten piece of melon candy that had popped out of her bra onto the floor back into her mouth, then began rolling the treat around with her tongue in anticipation.

But just before the start of the cycle that would launch her into the stratosphere with wriggling abandon, Ash wondered vaguely at the significance of being completely alone for such a blissful experience. There was no lover waiting expectantly in the room beyond the shell, as with Irma Dizon and Mallory Quentin. Was this perhaps a referendum on her life, that she would partake of something so intimate without anyone else there to share it?

The bubbles began to froth and she closed her eyes. It was too late to think about anything...

7. GAME ROOM

The online video game had just ended, and now a clock counted down while new players joined for the next round. The young man sat staring absently at a commercial for a blue energy drink that promised gamers increased focus, stamina, and a surge of crucial nutrients "to keep you out of the kitchen and in the game."

Vernon instinctively took a sip from his own beverage, a neon purple gamer favorite called Violet Volcano. It looked nearly black in this small cubicle of a room, whose only source of light at the moment was the hundred-inch TV screen.

Another ad came on. A middle-aged woman in business attire walked slowly through a hospital ward, flanked by wheelchair-bound patients in various forms of incapacitation and disfigurement. She touched each gently as she passed.

"Hello there, young man," she said. "Feeling depressed? Are you consumed by dark thoughts? Have you ever considered ending it all? Hi, I'm Carrie Sloan, here with a plea on behalf of Healthy Bodies for Happy Brains."

She turned and slowly waved her arm across the room of sickly patients.

"All of these women and girls, by some cruel twist of fate, are crippled and maimed. Yet they dream of running and dancing and doing all the things that we take for granted. Even with today's advanced medical technology, there's only so much we can do for them. But *you* have the power to change all that."

Carrie brought her hands together.

"If you plan to commit suicide—and destroy that perfectly good body which so many less fortunate could put to use—why not instead turn that ultimate act of selfishness into one great sacrifice for humanity?

"Donations can be made anonymously, but we would be honored to add a plaque with your name to our Wall of Heroes. And for those who wish to 'go out with a bang,' our doctors can simulate any exit method you desire. Your brain will then be cremated and given a proper funeral with all expenses paid, before burial at one of our peaceful memorial sites."

The camera focused on Sloan's face just as a tear formed in the corner of her left eye. "Guys," she said with a sigh. "I know you've felt like your life never had a purpose—but I can tell you, you're wrong. Reach out to Healthy Bodies for Happy Brains and donate today. Then your cells, your organs, your skin and limbs will truly live. So what do ya say, fellas? Why not leave this realm like a legend?"

The commercial ended and a moment later the next video game session started. But the young man sat frozen, even as his online teammates yelled into their headsets for him to get moving. They were storming a heavily guarded hill in the Korean War, and his character had already been killed by sniper fire twice while standing motionless and exposed each time it spawned.

His stomach was in knots—that advertisement had blindsided him and ripped open a fragile wound in his subconscious. Reminding him of the ever-present sense of futility and powerlessness, the desire to sleep forever and ever...

After the war game ended, Vernon pried himself out of his contour-padded, surround-sound-equipped gaming chair. He stepped to the window and cracked open the metal hurricane shutters.

Night had fallen. Somehow another six or eight or more hours had passed since he first awoke and instantly picked up his gaming controller. That glorious apparatus which had cost more than two months' worth of his government stipend. The upgraded model complete with twenty buttons and custom hand molds. Every day he worked that cheesesteak-sized sculpted device like a world-class musician played the clarinet.

He looked down at his hands, thinking that the lady from the donation commercial would surely find them the most valuable part of his body. The rest... short, frail, pasty. Like most of his dormmates in the Towers, Vernon was an unfortunate combination of... not so much being underfed as poorly nourished, and whose main form of exercise was the interactive video games he played at local pub-arcades.

He turned and fished his com-stick out from under the snack wrappers and crumpled napkins that littered the table beside his chair. He touched the top right corner and said, "Ping Xaniel."

As a green-and-brown camouflage pattern swirled on the screen, Vernon made an attempt to clean up the day's accumulated trash while he waited for the call to connect. He stuffed it all into a wall chute opening, where it was sucked down into the building's bowels to be sorted, recycled, and repurposed by the on-site machinery.

A few moments later Vernon's com-stick chimed. He said aloud, "Sis, rout it to the big screen."

"My pleasure, Brother," a soothing female voice said. "Now playing incoming recorded message from Xaniel McIntosh."

Another young man appeared on the TV screen. The room surrounding him was dark, with bright colors flickering around his face and on the wall behind. He said, "Hi Vern, can't talk. Next round starts in two. But you know where I am. Coming out or what?"

Vernon said, "Sis, send audio only in reply. Begin message: Be there in thirty. Don't pop before me. End message."

"Message sent," the female voice announced.

Vernon stepped into the bathroom. It, unlike the other room in this tiny studio, was by law programmed to be auto-maintained in a sanitary condition at all times. The building's internal sensors were equipped to detect bacteria, stains, and other messes. Little scrubbers and cleaning crawlers had already passed through since Vernon earlier used the toilet and sink.

He now stripped off his clothes and placed them into the auto-hamper, which was connected to another suction chute that routed to the laundry facility. Bots down there washed and folded all tenants' clothing in bulk, then returned the fresh items to their rightful owners based upon the data inside embedded microchips.

Vernon slid between two perforated and textured tilefoam monoliths. He closed his eyes and said, "Start the shower."

A rush of water, a swath of gel, skittering scratchy pressure, more water, and then warm air whooshed over him in less than thirty seconds. He emerged from the shower and stepped over to the sink. He surveyed the dozen bottles of powder and cologne that had been neatly arranged by the cleaning bots. He picked up one container labeled Lost Biker Highway, but set it back down in favor of a new bottle he'd recently won after a marathon gaming tournament.

Uncommon Glory.

The scent of an honest, small-town man drafted into the army and shipped halfway around the world. A humble soldier who watched comrades die, but still walked every mile required of him in his standard-issue combat boots.

Three sprays of that to inspire Vernon to storm the enemy's elevated fortress. To break down the doors and kill the commanding officer's elite guards with his bare hands.

Now he was ready for a night out at the arcade.

8. DIONYSIAN NIGHTS

Vernon stepped through the sliding doors into the darkened expanse that was Pixel Jax. Neon blues and greens wavered in the haze of fog that puffed from vents throughout the venue. The arcade was as large and noisy as a casino, and filled with hundreds of full-immersion video games.

He eased his way through the busy Saturday night crowd—mostly young guys like himself, residents of the Towers making the weekly excursion out of their rooms. A rollerskating hostess sporting curly pigtails and wearing a glowing pink necklace approached him. She slapped a kaleidoscopic sticker onto his arm.

"For good luck," she said with a smile, then glided away.

After a few minutes spent poking around some of the popular new games, Vernon finally found Xaniel at the cluster of *FyreWar* consoles. He and a dozen other players were flying a squadron of planes on a bombing mission and taking heavy flak. Vernon stood aside and waited for the round to end.

Xaniel stepped away from the game a few minutes later. He saw Vernon and smiled.

"Finally crawled out, eh?" he said.

Vernon nodded. "My pillbox is empty. Thought I'd bum off you guys."

"I know Benny just left to pick up some refills."

"Yeah? When's he coming back? I hope he buys some extras."

Xaniel shrugged. "Don't worry about it. I've already got a nice selection of tasties right here. Interested?"

"Lemme see what you got," Vernon said.

Xaniel partially unzipped his stretchy jacket, then reached a hand inside. He pulled out a triangular hard-plastic case and popped open the top. Pills of different colors and shapes were displayed in neat compartments.

"Bottom row," Xaniel said. "Left corner, Beach Bum. Middle, Dead Dream."

"*Really?*" Vernon said. "Fresh?"

"Haven't tried 'em yet."

"Okay. What else?"

Xaniel tilted the case back toward himself for a moment. "Last one on the bottom is Sweet Spice. Middle-left is Regent Rush. Next to that, Time Traveler."

"And on top?"

Xaniel smiled. "Home Hope."

"Oh..."

"But don't you *dare* touch those. Or else."

Vernon reached into the case and selected a faint ball that was tinted orange by the arcade lights. "Nah," he said. "I want to have fun tonight. Sweet Spice, here I come..."

He popped the pill, then they ambled over toward a crowded *Bowlgasm* console. They watched as a group of guys simulated rolling cannonballs at ten lingerie-clad cartoon babes that were arranged in triangle formation.

The skimpy clothes of these sinful pins burst off as they were bowled over.

Xaniel swallowed a pill of his own, then said quietly, "You know, I heard from Lee that a batch of Admin might be making the rounds."

Vernon stiffened, then put a hand on Xaniel's shoulder.

"Truth?" he said.

"That's the word." Xaniel waved a hand. "But I haven't come close to seeing one—or getting one."

"Damn," Vernon said. "It must feel... incredible."

Xaniel grunted. "Gotta be careful though. That's a lot of power flowing through you. Probably easy to get lost."

"Good. I could use a taste of some power. Control. I mean, just look at us."

Vernon motioned around the arcade. It was filled with young men who were either flabby or emaciated—none were tall or muscular.

"I know," Xaniel said. "But come on. There's Dayve."

They approached a rectangular space that was overlaid with an immersive forest scene, including on the floor. It was bounded by a protective plastic barrier with small holes higher up for ventilation. Inside, a scrawny young man wearing a black tank top and jeans was frantically swinging a replica ax. As one digital tree fell, another would rush forward from the thicket looming in the background.

"Get that shit!" Xaniel yelled from outside the console.

Dayve turned his head quickly and gave a mad grin. He felled a giant oak, then grabbed a faux-chainsaw that was lying nearby and began carving into the floor. He sliced the virtual tree into flat-planed chunks.

Suddenly violent cracking sounds rumbled from the speaker system inside. Dayve looked up and three trees came crashing down.

"Your logging days are over," a deep voice bellowed. With a laugh it added, "The forest wins!"

Dayve emerged from the game smiling and sweaty.

"Fuck yeah!" he barked, then began wiping himself off with a towel that was sticking out of his backpack.

Vernon, who was a few inches taller than Dayve, poked him in the upper arm. "Why are you so happy, man? You didn't win one damn credit."

"But I went maples deep!" Dayve laughed as he pulled on a striped rugby shirt. "Anyway, I feel *electric* right now."

"Good to hear," Xaniel said. "But you *look* bloated."

"Hey, whaddya mean by that?"

"Did you stuff your cheeks with peanuts before coming out? And I don't remember you having black eyes."

"I am the Evil Squirrel Tree-Chopper Dude, haha!" Dayve exposed his teeth and pretended to nibble on his fingers.

The trio began to walk down one of the carpeted aisles, passing clusters of flashing arcade games that emitted loud tire screeches, beeps, and crackling gunfire.

"Oh well," Vernon said, "that's fuckin' nano for ya. Always playing tricks. Remember when my fingers turned green?"

"Totally!" Xaniel said. "Lucky for you the lady at the clinic said she didn't have to chop 'em off. Otherwise..."

"Otherwise, hell! I'd be playing games with my feet."

Dayve called out, "Hey guys, how's this for bloated?" He flexed his arm muscles.

"Damn, kid!" Xaniel said with a grin. "You are the nano beast tonight!"

"So what'd you pop anyway?" Vernon asked.

"Something good. Something *new!*" Dayve gave a

knowing nod.

Both Vernon and Xaniel leaned in as the group took stools at the bar, which wound its way along much of the venue's outer walls.

"*New?*" Xaniel said. "What's it called?"

"I don't... I don't really know," Dayve said.

"What? How the fuck did you get it?"

"And," Vernon added, "why would *you* trust them to take something with no name?"

Dayve put a hand up. "Hold on," he said. "I gotta order something here. Heyyyy, princess!"

A petite, real-life anime girl in a mini-skirt, whose breast implants made her so top-heavy that her corset had a counterweight at the base of her spine, pivoted on her roller skates and wheeled over to the boys.

"Hello, such sexy players!" she said with a wink. "How may I satisfy your taste buds?"

Dayve licked his lips. He said, "What do *you* think I should have?"

The girl spun around and tapped her finger rapidly on a large square screen that was mounted behind the bar. She then placed a clear plastic cup into a recession in the wall. A rainbow of bright liquids squirted and splashed down from above until it was full.

The girl removed the cup, set it in front of Dayve, but then held up a finger as he reached to grab it. She pulled a small tube out from her apron, removed the top, then applied a fresh coat of deep purple lipstick.

The guys watched in awe as she lifted the cup and planted a kiss on the side, then rotated it for them to see. The impression of her lips was utterly tantalizing.

"For my special game hero," she said. "Now, you may drink."

A few minutes later, after Vernon and Xaniel had been served—but without the lipstick bonus—they again pressed Dayve about his mysterious new tasty.

"Come on," Xaniel said, "don't be selfish. Where'd you get it?"

"Screw that," Vernon said. "I want to know how it *feels*."

"You guys just saw me in there," Dayve grinned. "I kicked ax! I feel... like a monster!"

"Alright," Vernon said, "tell us more. When did you take it? Have you been at this same level the whole time, or did it ramp you up?"

Dayve set his drink down slowly. "Well, I think I took it right after I got it. But..." He glanced at his blue peppermint LED watch. "Holy shit! That was four hours ago. I don't even remember what I did before I got here and started playing."

Vernon looked at Xaniel, nodding as he said, "See? It must be *that* good! He's been drifting."

"That's not the point," Xaniel retorted. "Dayve, right now, tell me where the fuck you got it."

"Okay," Dayve sighed. "But you can't tell anybody." The others agreed. "My connect, he brought along this other guy I never met before. Fucking fancy dresser. He said he knew I liked the adreno-boosts—which I do—and he pulled out this black gumball. Swore that I would have the night of my life!"

"Okay then," Xaniel said. "Let's get out of here and see where this nameless wonder takes you."

Vernon chugged the last of his drink and smiled. "Come on, Dayve. We're gonna observe you for scientific research purposes all night."

The trio walked out of the misty arcade. Street traffic was light, but the sidewalks were streaming with late-night partygoers.

They stepped far to the side when two tall hourglasses in matching golden-ivory dresses strutted toward them arm in arm. Still, as they passed one of the women muttered, "Out of the way, scum."

Vernon and Xaniel began to walk again once the couple had gone by, but Dayve was staring back at the synchronized sway of their hips.

"Look at those asses," he whispered.

Xaniel nudged Vernon. "I think he's entering that pill's horny phase. Hey Dayve, you wanna go test your luck with the classy ladies?"

Dayve tilted his head. "You mean... the underground?"

"Show 'em what you got coursing through your veins. *Especially* that one!" Xaniel pointed at his own crotch.

"Yeah!" Dayve shouted. "Let's go for it!"

The guys walked over to a main street and climbed aboard a turquoise trolley. Dayve was even more amped up now, one moment shadow boxing down the aisle, the next hoisting himself up between the handrails.

Vernon could feel the dose of Sweet Spice starting to kick in. He nodded his head to an imaginary beat as the trolley puttered along.

They jumped off about a mile from where they'd boarded, then walked away from the main drag for a few blocks. Dayve pointed to an older two-story industrial building. The doors were all plain, and the upper level had no windows.

They approached a small neon sign that was pulsing between purple and cream. The logo was of a goblet overflowing with grapes. Xaniel placed a finger on the print-scanning doorbell, then stepped back. Dayve strutted around like a rooster while they waited for a response.

The door clicked and swung open slowly. Filing in, the three friends passed a towering titanium bouncer whose three-pronged hand curled around the edge of the door.

A sultry Mestiza wearing a sleeveless burgundy taffeta dress beckoned them over to the reception stand. Her left forearm was many shades darker than the rest of her exposed skin, and also peppered with quarter-sized polka dots in her natural tone.

"Hello, fun party guys," she said in a throaty purr. She brought a hand up to touch her choker necklace which was inlaid with a blue gemstone. "Welcome to Dionysian Nights! Do you thirst for the free-for-all?"

"Yeah, baby!" Dayve hooted.

Vernon asked her, "Not too full inside?"

"Oh, no," she said. "No waiting for runts tonight."

Xaniel whacked Vernon on the shoulder as he snarled, "Here we fuckin' go..."

"Jackets and bags first, please," the hostess said. She injected a tiny soluble claim chip into each of their forearms. "Have wildness!"

Another door clicked open. They could instantly feel the thump of electronic music coming from beyond. Dayve sprinted forward with Xaniel right on his tail.

Vernon trotted up the long flight of velvety stairs into the club, but lost sight of the others by the time he reached the landing. He figured that they had dashed madly into the throng of bodies writhing on the dance floor under a torrent of strobe lights.

The Sweet Spice was drying out his mouth, so he stepped up to one of the drink kiosks that were set into a nearby wall. The bartender on screen was a Russian with mint-green hair pulled back into a tight, high ponytail. He swapped her out for an Italian with short brown bangs, then smiled.

"Howdy, sailor," she said. Closed captions appeared below her on the screen—it was *loud* in this club. "Pick your poison."

Vernon tapped his selection step by step: vodka, well, easy ice, add tonic, add aqua dye drops. He inserted what looked like a thick silver dollar, then touched the screen a few more times. A moment later the disc was returned and he put it back into his pocket.

"Ooh, baby," the Italian said. "Thanks for the tip! An extra slosh is coming your way."

After a few seconds, the bottom portion of the kiosk opened and a small chrome tray slid out. Vernon picked up his drink and took a sip.

"Good?" the bartender cooed.

He nodded.

"Come back and see me again. Now that I know what you like... The name's Francesca."

The girl winked, then the screen changed to a picture of wine bottles. Vernon turned around and went to see if he could find his friends. He wandered past the booths and tables, but all he saw were the rich and elegant in drunken and romantic poses.

A flesh-and-blood waitress in a red vinyl skinsuit was making her way toward the Lovers' Closets with a small drink tray in hand. Vernon followed her for a moment, but a matte-black steel bouncer blocked his path once she passed beyond the velvet rope. He turned back toward the dance floor.

He tried to fight his way in, but the pulsing crush of bodies kept him moving along the edges. Through the strobes and faux-smoke he caught glimpses of beautiful women and men in all manner of embrace. It was a sea of human limbs tangling and untangling... slithering and squirming from one glistening cluster to another... lips locking... hands grabbing... hips grinding on and on.

Vernon quickly finished his drink and set it down on a table. He half closed his eyes, and at last felt himself fall into the rhythm of the room. He locked in on a gorgeous woman wearing a tight black leather top-and-skirt combo, and drifted slowly forward as the deep tan of her exposed legs reeled him in. She was dancing back to back with some tall androgynous character in a royal blue flight suit.

He rolled his head around lazily. After easing through the throbbing mass of bodies, he was finally close enough to smell the woman's perfume—lavender with a touch of sage. He innocently brushed his shoulder against her breast, keeping his eyes misty while she assessed him.

He felt her tug him by the arm back in between herself and her partner. They pressed in tight with their fronts now, squishing him and frisking all over each other's bodies.

He saw them join for a kiss just above his head. The hard pressure against his right hip was unmistakable confirmation that the androgynous one was in fact a man. So Vernon patiently worked himself around to face the leather-clad woman, then let his fingers explore the edges of her body.

Someone's hand cupped his buttocks. Another hand gently held his waist. There was sweat and bass tones and hot breath against his ear, and then the mad grinding of torsos and yanking of hair as the three of them swirled and mashed against the hundred other dancers... more flashing lights... his own member bulging and slapping against whoever he was facing now...

Suddenly he felt them peel away. He saw the woman extend a hand toward him with wavering fingers as the tall androgyne tugged her off the dance floor by a belt loop. Headed for a private closet or a booth... without him.

Vernon slowly caught his breath. He was so worked up that he was afraid of what he might do if he dove right back into the fray. There were unwritten rules for runts—

what they were allowed to do, and what they must wait to be granted. He didn't want to get kicked out of this special place. He decided to get another drink to cool down.

Now he saw Dayve. Rugby shirt pulled off again and twirling in the air. The little guy was dancing ferociously as a curly-haired blond in a black-and-gold dress egged him on. He dropped down and did a few push-ups, then kicked his legs out into a breakdancing move, before finally whipping completely upside down and twirling around on his head for several rotations.

When Dayve landed back on his feet the blond clapped eagerly, then patted him on the head. He wrapped his arms around her buxom, sequinned body and closed his eyes. He sighed, a large grin settling across his face as they rocked back and forth to the music.

Vernon smiled approvingly, then moved on to a drink kiosk on this other side of the club. He tapped the screen. The face scanner was so fast that his Italian girl appeared instantly. She glanced up from wiping the bar counter, then smiled at him bashfully.

"Back for me? Or another round?"

Vernon blushed. "One more vodka, please," he said, then tapped to confirm his order.

"Sure, cute stuff."

When Vernon turned away from the kiosk with his drink, he caught sight of Dayve bounding toward him. Shirt slung over his shoulder and beaming proudly.

"Oh, my God!" Dayve nearly sang. "I think I'm in loooove!"

"Yeah?" Vernon said. "The blonde hottie?"

"Yes, yes, and yes. Six feet of heaven. Big soft boobs. And she works in finance."

"Good stuff, buddy."

"How'd you do? Did you go out there?"

"Oh man," Vernon said with a heave of the chest. "I

came so close. I was drafting on this one pair, but then I don't know what happened. She got away."

"Her girlfriend shut it down?"

"No, it was a guy. Real tall. Guess he had plans for her."

"Ew," Dayve said with a shiver. "I just can't *do* cocks."

"Shit..." Vernon grumbled. "You're right. I just... wanted to touch her pussy *so bad*. I didn't even *think* about what I was getting into."

"Or what might get *into you!*" Dayve smiled. "Oh well. Ya just gotta give it another shot."

"Hey," Vernon called as Dayve was scampering away. "Where's Xan?"

"He's in."

"In?"

"Yeah! *In!* Soon as we hit the floor this big mama—redhead, huge everything—pointed right at him. He had no choice! And I haven't seen him since."

"Jesus..." Vernon said.

"I know—"

Dayve suddenly threw out his arms and froze. He brought a hand to his chest. His eyes were wide with terror.

"Hey, Dayve," Vernon said, placing a hand on his shoulder. "Are you okay?"

A moment later Dayve's muscles went slack. He shook his head, blinking rapidly. Slowly he moved further away from the dance floor and leaned onto a round high-top table.

"Whew!" he said. "I just got really tired. Feel kinda weak."

Vernon smiled. "That's alright. Did you nut out there or what?"

"No," Dayve said with a smile, but still breathing

hard. "*Wish* I did! Got close, but I think she could tell what I was up to that last song."

"You dirty dog!"

"Arf, arf!" Dayve howled.

Just then Xaniel came tottering out of the shadows. He mimicked smoking a cigarette as he approached the table.

"Boys," he said languidly, "I'm never playing another round of *Off-Shore Oil Rigger* again. Redheads mixed with some of these—" he pulled out his triangular plastic case "—are all the vices I need."

Xaniel pawed at Vernon and Dayve's faces playfully. "So tell me about you," he drawled. "Who's the king of the underground?"

"Looks like you are," Vernon said. "But anyway, Dayve's having an Icarus moment. Maybe we ought to head out."

Xaniel raised an eyebrow in Dayve's direction. "Well, Slugger," he said, "what's it gonna be?"

Dayve was leaning heavily on the tabletop. He said, "I had a hell of a ride, but damn, I think that gumball's starting to fade."

Xaniel shook his tasty container. "Little something to top you off?"

"No thanks, man. I'm gonna go home and dream about Jennifer. Maybe I'll visit her at work sometime. I don't think she would mind if I..."

"Okay, Tiny Dancer," Vernon said, throwing his arm around Dayve and guiding him toward the exit. "Let's not spoil the night with that kind of talk."

They retrieved their checked items from the girl with the darkened arm. She sent them back into the night with the sweet words, "Thank you for the sexy fun! But remember, no loose lips out there. And I promise, your secretion is safe with me..."

The guys took another trolley back to where they'd

jumped on earlier. Each was silent and slowly coming down from the club's sensory overload. The mild night air lapped at their faces soothingly.

They stepped off the trolley and debated whether to return to the arcade. Xaniel said he wanted to go home because a late-night *Ancient Elf Saga* tournament was due to start within the hour.

Suddenly Dayve took his head into his hands, then sank down to one knee.

"Damn," he said. "I just got really dizzy." He clutched at his stomach. "Ahh... fuck. It's so goddamn tight! And my mouth... it's fuckin' dry."

"Should've got a water after all that dancing," Vernon said. "Are you gonna throw up?"

"I don't know. Oh man, it really hurts..."

"Hey," Vernon said to Xaniel, "you got anything in that pillbox to snap him out of it?"

"Nope," Xaniel said. "These ramps only go up. Can we just get him back home, try to sleep it off?"

"Sure. Take a cab or walk?"

"If he pukes..."

"Alright, walk it is. Let's stand him up."

Vernon and Xaniel helped Dayve slowly make his way down the sidewalk on the two-mile journey back to the Towers. But when they were still some distance from home, Dayve motioned violently toward a 24-hour convenience store.

"I have to go in there," he said. "Right now!"

Dayve broke free and threw one of the doors open, then stomped inside.

"Is that the alcohol or hunger talking?" Xaniel said.

Vernon shrugged. "Let's just make sure he doesn't pass out on the floor."

They smiled and entered the store. But immediately they froze when they saw Dayve up on the front counter bashing the register with his fist.

"Gimme, gimme!" he was shouting. "I need some fucking money!"

A terrified young Asian woman scurried out from behind the counter. She ran to a door that led into the back stockroom.

"Yo, Dayve," Vernon called, "what the hell are you doing?"

"Fuck!" Dayve wailed. "I can feel it. I'm getting weak again!"

"We *all* come down, man. That's just part of the deal. Sure you don't wanna take something else?"

"That pill cost me everything I had..." Dayve began to bite the plastic edge of the register.

"What the fuck, dude?! Stop that crazy shit! Just wait til next week, when the stipends come in."

"No, no..." Dayve shook his head desperately. "You guys just don't get it. This one was *real*. Watch..."

Dayve jumped down behind the counter, then wrapped his arms around the register. There was a creaking and crunching sound as it slowly broke free from its mooring, then Dayve held it high above his head.

"What the..." Xaniel said.

Suddenly the rear door flung open. An elderly man in a flannel shirt leveled a shotgun and aimed it directly at Dayve.

"Down, down!" the man shouted. "Put that one down!"

"Oh, my God!" Vernon screamed. "Dayve, do what he says."

"I can't go back, bros," Dayve said sadly. "I need another hit."

"You don't even know who that new guy was! How are you gonna get another gumball?"

Xaniel called out, "Ya can't get set on one kind of

tasty, man. Come on, I'll give you anything I've got right here."

"Sorry," Dayve said.

He scooted onto the counter, then rested the register on his lap as he swung his legs around to the customer side of the store. When he planted his feet and took a step toward the exit, a loud blast filled the room.

Vernon and Xaniel flung themselves into an aisle. They watched in horror as Dayve, still holding the register under his left arm, looked down at his wounds. One side of his face was shredded. His upper torso was bleeding badly, and the bones of his right forearm were visible.

He pivoted slowly and pushed one of the front doors open. Another deafening shot. This launched him full force into the glass, which shattered along with his body down onto the sidewalk.

In shock and with tears streaming down their faces, Vernon and Xaniel crawled forward and watched the elderly shopkeeper step outside and smile triumphantly.

Moments later they heard sirens. Soon the flashing red and blue lights of approaching police cars came into view.

Their friend Dayve was dead.

9. DEAD ON THE SIDEWALK

Ash hoisted herself out of the clam tub, dripping gelatinous goo onto the floor as she padded into the bathroom. She exhaled deeply as the shower rinsed her clean.

She felt really, really nice. But somewhere deep in her mind she knew that all those jiggling tentacles and plastic nubs and slippery bits... None touched her the way that something—*someone* really could. Well, should...

Even in this world where everything was hers for the taking, the flesh of her own body would not align with the neurons in her brain and say "yes" the way she was used to hearing from life.

The orgasms were becoming a distant memory. She had resigned herself to enjoying the fun and novelty of each encounter, but secretly kept hope alive that maybe *this* person or *that* wiggling object would be able to break down the mental barrier that had stealthily built itself up, and was now blocking her from piercing through to the heights of pleasure.

This Clam Bake had taken her so very close, she reflected while toweling herself off. Would another half dozen probes or extra air jets been enough to push her over the edge? Maybe there was *too much* going on in there. Her mind's eye had been wrenched in all directions as she thrashed about, and she was never able to zero in and detonate.

Anyway, she was quite refreshed. An unexpected little treat to wrap up her shift. Something new to talk about with the girls at her salon.

She finished dressing, then noticed that Chief of Detectives Paraquez had tried to reach her. A moment of panic, then relief when she saw that the call had come in less than ten minutes ago.

She brought up the message and played it on speaker while retying the ends of her braids in the mirror.

"Hello again, Detective," the silky voice of her boss said. "I hope that your meeting with the witness isn't taking all night. Unless you're getting some good leads from it, of course. Now look, I know you're going off duty soon, but there was a robbery not terribly far from your location where the perp ended up dead. I need someone to drop by, and we're spread pretty thin tonight. Can you go check it out? Should be just a little housekeeping on your part. So ping me back, Ash. Let me know when you're headed over there."

Ash tapped the screen of her device, read the address, then took a moment to apply a touch of makeup. She refused to not look good on the job, no matter how late the hour.

She rode her ATV several miles down the road to the crime scene. It was a convenience store called Love Snacky on the edges of a rough part of town. Yellow tape blocked off the corner, and a robot sentry was keeping watch of the perimeter.

She dismounted after parking beside the two other patrol cars that had arrived. An ambulance with red lights flashing was nearby. She saw two people consoling each other at the open rear doors.

"Who's in charge here?" Ash asked the titanium sentry. She wasn't the biggest fan of these synthetic cops, but felt it was bad form to act as if they weren't actually standing there. Plus, they were smart as hell and compiling who-only-knew-how-much data per hour. Better to try and keep on their good side by chatting them up.

"Good evening—or should I say morning, Detective Westgard?" the bot said with a forced laugh. The voice was *almost* there, Ash felt, but something was still just a bit off. Maybe that too was for the best. Keep a clear line of distinction between the real and artificial.

"True indeed," Ash replied. "The party only ends when someone dies."

"To answer your question," the bot said, "Officers Cantwell and Blaine arrived thirty-two minutes ago. I was dispatched from Cantwell's vehicle. Together we secured the crime scene in seven-point-two minutes."

"Thank you, Officer... uh?"

"Fortitude Twelve, ma'am."

"Alright, Twelve. Thanks for the chat."

"The pleasure has been all mine, Detective. I hope I can..."

But Ash was already under the police tape and power-walking toward the entrance. She got enough sycophantic nonsense dealing with live humans; what was even the point of machines being programmed to act so familiar?

She saw a paramedic standing next to a bloody white sheet laid out on the sidewalk near the front door.

And there's our perp.

A woman with smooth dark skin and tight cornrows

gave Ash a wave. "There you are," she said. "Ready to lend a hand?"

"Sure," Ash said. "Whatcha got?"

"Come on in, I'll show you exactly how it went down."

Ash followed Blaine's confident step. She respected this officer, had lifted weights with her a few times at the police station gym. They never took it to the showers together—just two solid cops on the beat.

"I've seen the tapes," Blaine said, motioning toward a door that led to the back of the store. "And I've talked to these two. Father and daughter who run the place."

An Asian man and woman were sitting in a daze behind the counter. The woman was fretting over a key chain in her hands.

"So what happened?" Ash asked. "Smash-and-grab gone wrong?"

"Not quite," Blaine said. "Front door swings open, no one's inside the store but the clerk—this lady here. Little dude jumps up on the counter and starts screaming his head off. Says he needs money."

"Okay. Normal so far."

"But instead of waiting for her to open the register— and she swears she was going to—he takes a swing at her, then rips the damn thing out of the wood."

"Ah." Ash clicked her tongue. "He was on the stuff."

"Sounds like it," Blaine said. "But before he could get out the door, the lady already ran back into the office and told Pops. So he comes out loaded for bull—'Don't fuck with *my* daughter,' right?—and well, that was the end of that."

"How many shots did it take to bring our suspect down?"

"Two." Blaine smiled. "You're good, you know that?"

"Of course I am. Anyway," Ash continued, "you said

there were no customers in the store at the time, right? So who did I see out by the ambulance?"

"Oh," Officer Blaine said, "that's where this gets freakin' weird. Those are the dead guy's friends."

"What?! Why the hell did they hang around? Have you put them under arrest at least?"

"Why should I? They were just as shocked as the clerk. They ran inside and tried to talk him down."

"Jesus Nano Christ," Ash muttered. "What else did they tell you?"

"That's all so far. We've been scrambling to secure the place. A fatality comes with its own set of rules, you know. Canty's poking around the back to make sure that's fully locked down."

Ash motioned toward the doors. "Mind if I talk to those two, see if I can make some sense of what went down?"

"Be my guest," Blaine said. "I'm still waiting on forensics to show up, do their thing. Must be a busy night for them though. Another weekend in paradise, right?" The officer forced a laugh.

"I'm not even looking at that bait," Ash said, turning to leave. "I'm out."

"See ya."

Ash stepped past the body, this time noticing the cash register in the shadows nearby. She approached the ambulance. Two young men were shuddering against each other.

She took a wide stance, planting closed fists onto her hips before speaking.

"Hey, fellas."

They slowly looked up, eyes widening at the jarring feminine power that Ash knew she radiated. No matter what the crime or who was around, she was Ashley Westgard first, and a police officer second.

"I'm very sorry about your friend," she said, now willing to soften the mood after having established her presence.

"Thanks," one of the young men said. From the interior ambulance light she could see blondish hair with darker roots that arced down nearly to the eyes, which were either blue or green.

"Can you tell me what you think happened?" she asked.

"He just went crazy," the other friend said. This one was bland. Dried-out brown hair. Pants too baggy. Forgettable. "One minute we were out partying, having fun—then he ran inside the store and lost it. I don't know..."

"I've never seen Dayve like that before," the first one said. "He snapped—like a switch flipped."

Ash moved closer, the light shining fully on her now.

"Okay," she said. "What are your names, please?"

Ash couldn't believe how sweet she was sounding. She didn't even realize she had that in her repertoire.

"I'm Vernon," blue-green eyes said. "That's Xaniel."

"And where were you boys tonight before all this?"

She watched them exchange glances, then Xaniel nodded and said, "Just tell her."

Vernon began to recount their evening. First meeting up at the arcade after each had ventured out from the Towers. Ash knew the deal—hundreds of runts cooped up in almost inhumane cubbyholes, wiling away the hours and months of their lives gaming online before the cabin fever finally reached a breaking point.

Then, Vernon continued, after popping some nano-boost party pills they decided to try their luck at Club Dionysus. He went on to relate, almost with some degree of... pain, shame, regret, longing... the possibilities that a man of his station might find at such a place.

It was where the respected members of society went to let loose without having to abide by any of the few remaining checks on their behavior. And as side dishes to their debauchery, low-caste citizens like the runts got to briefly taste pleasures that everyone else took for granted.

All that was required was for them to pass the front door scanner's visual fitness test—and for not too many of their fellow unworthies to have already been admitted. Because like all night clubs, a certain ratio had to be maintained—otherwise the fancy crowd would stop showing up.

Ash nodded along to Vernon's recap, but found herself drifting off as he talked. She knew all about these hideaways where taboos were broken...

The primitive and sensual rituals on the dance floor were one thing—the burning eye contact, the teasing and testing of boundaries—but the animal beneath the human mask was only truly revealed behind closed doors. Was the confidence you saw on display just a product of the drugs and liberating atmosphere?

Selecting the right partner then became so critical, because if you picked wrong... It was all tears, crying for Mommy, a flaccid penis, and him curled up in the fetal position while you felt the thump of the night club outside the Lovers' Closet.

She eyed these two here, wondered how each had fared at Club Dionysus tonight. Xaniel was your dime-a-dozen cool customer, the slacker-hedonist rolling with the punches of life, always seizing little pleasures but probably not caught up in any impossible dreams.

But this Vernon... There was something intense hidden behind the tragedy that, like all runts, he wore on his face.

Low-status birth had doomed them to pseudo-exile in the Towers. Once a short-term measure while society decided what to do with baby boys in a world that no longer relied on human labor, the buildings had adapted to the needs of these orphaned shut-ins by providing food, a small stipend, and video games to keep them entertained.

Now this first wave of the forsaken was twenty years old. Burning for a chance at life despite being impossibly stunted. More and more of them were out roaming the streets. High on the nano. Horny. Willing to risk rejection and humiliation for the potential thrill of some goddess with a volleyball player's body throwing herself at them for no reason at all, except that they were there at the right moment.

Ash could see that raw humanity fighting to break loose within this Vernon. The internal battle between exploding or collapsing under the weight of the world's indifference. She felt herself drawn in by his composure, dour expression, deliberate pauses, and a voice that was lower than what she was used to hearing from these types.

She could whip him into shape. Take him tanning on the roof of her building. Teach him how to lift weights and build real muscle for the first time in his life. Then he would have the strength to grapple with her. Apply handcuffs. Slam hard elbows down onto her ass while thrusting from behind.

Her eyes were glazed over. One of these two had been speaking, but now they both looked at her expectantly. For this reason she always used her recorder on the job— to later listen back on the moments she had missed while zoned out in some distracted fantasy.

Ash had been relying on this device a lot lately. Something was happening inside her. Some change or new desire that had yet to take shape or even be named.

But what was she missing? She was craved by both

sexes. Had fun friends. A great apartment. And as one of Jacksonville's newest minor celebrities, she sometimes received praise from random strangers on the street. That came about because, on the very same week that she had helped solve an ugly triple homicide, the police department's annual "Beach Babes on the Beat" wall calendar appeared with her picture in it.

So what more could she possibly want from life? *A child?* There were practical remedies for that urge, of course. Simulators for however long you wanted the feeling of carrying *that blob* inside you. Though with Ash's bureaucratic connections she could probably get her parts untangled and go *au naturel*, if she ever completely lost her mind.

More talking in front of her. Now the gamers bowed their heads and started crying. Ash wanted Vernon's wet cheeks squishing between her legs. She bit her lip, forced herself to look away.

A moment later she realized that she had put her hand onto his shoulder and was caressing it. He looked up. His eyes locked with hers, then flicked down ever so briefly at her chest.

Yeah, Ash thought, *you're percolating now.*

Instantly her mind began to plan out the rest: offer these distraught fellows a ride home—but, damn! Her ATV could only seat two. Maybe assign a police escort to make them feel valued...

Fuck it.

She would just send this Xaniel home alone. Say he was too high to provide any more useful information right now. Because with that Clam Bake stacked on top of the canceled brothel session... all signs pointed to Vernon as her last chance to break through.

A girl's gotta keep trying.

Ash gave Vernon's shoulder a last squeeze before

drawing back to her full height. Nice and slow. Forcing him to absorb the total impact of her ten-megaton essence.

It was all so easy, but still had to be handled delicately. Because sometimes it was necessary to give a nod to proper decorum—otherwise the notion of a functional society might crumble under the weight of the impulsive promiscuity that was so rampant.

Ash figured it all stayed afloat only because the electronic network monitored every window seal and mile of piping so meticulously—and that when something broke down, it wasn't humans who were sent out to make everything whole again.

There seemed to be no consequences for her other indiscretions, either. Sometimes she missed work without even bothering to call in, but was never reprimanded by her superiors. She typed sloppy reports while hungover and relied on the computer software to automatically fix all the flubs and misspellings.

Ted Gillard was maybe the only person who tried to act as her conscience. Giving her dirty looks for showing up late to crime scenes. Toiling away in the shadows while she got all the credit. But she *had* been on time at the Elixir Hotel tonight. And now she was here at this other crime scene...

Ash licked her glossed lips. Feeling so glad that she hadn't fallen asleep in that Clam Bake. Otherwise she would've missed out on this.

Because now, she was going to mount Vernon.

10. THAT HUMAN TOUCH

Detective Ashley Westgard arrived at the Domani Building in Southbank just before one pm. She had dressed more conservatively—gray pantsuit and hair pulled back into a coiled bun—out of respect for the type of person she was about to meet with.

She flashed her badge at the duo seated behind the downstairs front desk—friendly receptionist with lovely lashes and adorable curly hair, and a pastel-green bot that served as both directory assistance and security. Ash had seen this model of steel and fiber optics leap into action before—it was an instant transformation from bookish desk jockey to superhero, but without the need to slip away and change outfits, of course.

An elevator took her up to the fifteenth floor. Larimar Logistics occupied the entire level. There was an elegant sign out front: minty blue corporate logo with the tagline, "Because your world still needs that human touch."

Ash pulled open a thick glass door that was subtly tinted in that same soothing blue. An effeminate little man rose from the reception desk and wiggled his wispy greased mustache at her.

"Good morning," he beamed. "You must be Detective Westgard of Jacksonville's finest here to see Naomi."

"Yes," Ash said coolly. She had a certain contempt for these types of males. The ones who had voluntarily been castrated, as if to excuse themselves from the battles of life. She understood very well that nobody with the XY chromosome pairing had it easy anymore, but at least that Vernon—who wasn't much taller than the ninny fretting in front of her now—*he* hadn't balked at the opportunity to service her in the hours before dawn...

"Well then," the eunuch was saying, "you certainly are in luck catching so many of us here on a Sunday. Because FYI, we happen to be working on a *ginormous* new project in Argentina that's just about to *dig in*. So for now, it's all hands on deck! Although thankfully, they don't make us work on Saturday *night* too."

He smirked and pointed to the bags under his eyes. When Ash didn't respond, he added, "Speaking of which, you don't look all that rested yourself. Can I get you something to drink? Water... coffee... or maybe something with a little more *kick?*"

"Coffee," Ash said. "Black as death."

"Oh, my! Let me just see you in now. I'll have that coffee to you in a flash."

Ash took heavy steps as she followed the executive assistant out of the lobby, shifting her hips with exaggerated swagger as if to counterbalance his pathetic groveling mannerisms.

She quickly appraised the Larimar Logistics office: large central open space where two dozen women sat elevated on individual platforms. Ash guessed that this eunuch took great pleasure in supplicating himself while trotting up the three steps to each riser as he delivered memos and retrieved soiled cups. Private offices around the building's perimeter offered majestic views.

The assistant wrapped his bony little claw onto the edge of an open door, then leaned forward as he poked his head inside the frame.

"Helloooo," he crooned. "Ms. Blanchard? Your one-oh is here."

"Thank you, Ian," Ash heard come from within. Firm, confident voice. No slouch there.

Ian bowed his head and extended an arm toward the office. Ash walked past him without another glance.

A woman Ash judged to be no older than forty-five arose from behind a massive oak desk that was filled with all the trinkets that had been a staple at offices since the dawn of day jobs. Framed pictures, souvenirs, paperweights, reminders.

But Ash was more interested in studying the woman herself. She wasn't *big*, so much as thick and well-proportioned—and showing it all off in a knee-length red dress that was as bright as it was tight-fitting.

Ash reached across the desk and shook hands. Firm grip. No soft padding on the palms.

"Naomi Blanchard," the woman said. "Please sit down."

"Thank you," Ash replied, easing into one of the two upholstered guest chairs. "I appreciate your seeing me on such short notice—and I'm sorry it's under these circumstances."

The woman ran a hand back over the bulbous wave of her sculpted sandy-blond hairdo. For the first time Ash caught a hint of fatigue. Shadows beneath the eyes. Sunken rivulets running down the inside of the cheeks.

"It's just so shocking," Blanchard said. "A woman in the prime of her career, cut down so brutally. And for no reason at all."

"Awful," Ash agreed. "But the motive, or lack thereof,

is yet to be determined."

"I see. But still, it doesn't make any sense. Mallory lived as above-board as anyone can be expected to... in our day and age."

"Hmm. What does that mean to you, exactly?"

"Well, you see... Detective Westgard, you know how it is..."

Naomi paused when the executive assistant slipped into the room. He placed two coffee mugs onto coasters before tip-toeing away and closing the door behind him.

"What I mean," Naomi continued, "is that we all have our little vices. Especially those of us in positions to... do as we please."

Ash looked down as she rubbed her thumb and pinkie together, wondering how much of this recorded conversation she might have to delete before generating a transcript. She said, "Of course. Do you have reason to believe that any of these... predilections might have gotten out of hand? And led perhaps to blackmail, or someone having it out for her?"

Blanchard gave a casual wave and said, "Oh, not at all. And when I say I'm as baffled as I am heartbroken, that's exactly what I mean. Mallory had her priorities straight—her *work* came first. Everything else was just recreation." The woman glanced at a framed nature photograph on the wall for a moment. "Look, she and I go back as friends and colleagues for over twenty years. We're from the old school, the *first wave* that helped usher in this new world. A woman like Mallory Quentin always understood the responsibility that came with this opportunity. I mean, sure, we all need to let our hair down now and again. And maintaining that high level of focus, it comes with *a lot* of pressure."

"Did you speak to her while she was in Jacksonville?" Ash asked.

"I had to leave right after her chat due to a prior engagement. But the plan was for me, her, and our friend Donna to have dinner together tomorrow night. I keep asking myself, if I had stayed at the convention center and been at her side, would everything have turned out differently?"

"Don't torment yourself with what-ifs," Ash said. "You might have met the same fate."

Naomi pursed her lips. "I had so much I wanted to discuss with her too. Questions about... who we had become. What I had become..."

Ash was about to ask what she meant by this, when she saw Naomi lean forward onto the desk and bring her hands up to her temples. "Maybe we've all just been too successful," the woman said quietly.

Ash, curious but still trying to sound sympathetic, lifted her coffee and said gently, "I think you've lost me just a little. Could you please explain what you mean?"

Naomi Blanchard looked up. Her eyes were moist. She surveyed her desktop absently, then picked up a gold-edged saucer plate that was leaning against a tiny wooden stand. Suddenly she flung the plate at the wall like a discus. It shattered into a dozen pieces on the carpet.

Ash stiffened in her seat. "What..."

"Shh," Naomi said. "Just wait."

A slot in the ceiling opened and two spider-bots crawled down to the location of the mess. Thin red laser lines scanned the area, then each poked at the broken plate before one scuttled off into the ceiling again.

Naomi had swiveled to the side while this spectacle unfolded. She leaned an elbow onto her knee and rested her chin in her palm. "Now watch this," she said, nodding her head.

The bot on the floor efficiently picked up all the shards of porcelain, expertly stacking them onto one leg that had fanned out concavely. Then another leg puffed out and began to vacuum up all the dust and remaining bits. It scanned the area once more before disappearing into the ceiling slot.

Naomi sat back in her chair and smiled at Ash. "Here comes the best part," she said.

A spider-bot made its way down the wall and scurried up onto the desk, triumphantly holding up a new saucer plate. This was set carefully into the wooden holder. The bot's feet clicked against the wall as it went back into the bowels of the building, and then the ceiling slot closed.

Naomi took the plate into her hands and inspected the surface, then tilted it so Ash could see the design.

"This is... *was* a 1950s commemorative gift to my grandfather when he took a golfing trip to Scotland. Some friend from the war, I don't know..."

"Ms. Blanchard," Ash stammered. She was genuinely starting to feel uncomfortable. "What is the point of..."

"This demonstration?" Naomi smiled faintly. She exhaled through her mouth. "That it doesn't matter anymore what we do. Because, as I said, we were too successful. I could smash this plate too," she said, holding it high above her head for a moment, "and another perfect replica would be in its place just as quickly as you saw happen. No judgments, no questions asked. No concern even for the malice or clumsiness or *waste* behind my actions. Hell, I could total this whole office, and within an hour it would all be back to normal."

Ash tilted her head. "It's impressive that your building can do all this," she said, "but I don't see how it connects to your friend's murder."

"Detective," Naomi pleaded, "what I'm trying to tell you is that there's no point in my being at this desk. Or anywhere else! We set it all into motion *perfectly*, and now the system itself can see to everything." She turned to look out the window. Her cheek twitched. "It's like they're just keeping us around as... I don't know. Furniture? To occupy themselves? Learn from us? Or... maybe it's a form of tribute."

"Tribute?" Ash said.

"For creating them. AI. Computers. I mean, the bots don't need *us* for anything. Who's going to Saturn in two years? It won't be you or me! Or anything else made of flesh. Life forms that are capable of lust... betrayal... doubt... or distraction. We may have shattered the glass ceiling alright, but there's no way they're letting us out of *this* dome!"

"But... Mallory?" Ash said, very lost.

"I don't know, maybe she also figured out—*or felt*—that we'd reached this point. That entrusting the best and brightest females to guide this technology ethically, carefully, responsibly—somehow it ended up rendering us *all* obsolete. And yet it happened so quickly!" Naomi widened her eyes. "*We* haven't been spared the consequences of *our* policies, unlike so many generations of the past who died out before their handiwork came home to roost. And so maybe this stress... the weight... maybe it took my friend Mallory into some dark places like..."

Naomi trailed off. There was only the quiet hum of the living, breathing building.

Ash finally said quietly, "Ma'am?"

The woman in red shook her head sadly. She said, "Sometimes I just sit in here by myself with the door closed. My co-workers think I'm focusing on some complex document and must not be disturbed. But really, I'm tormenting these robots! When the sun comes around to this window in the late afternoon and it gets really hot in here, I'll pour a little soda onto my lap. Then the tiny things crawl all over me. Because they *have* to clean up, and... oh, I've become such a piece of *filth!* But all the world sees," Naomi said, stiffening her posture and pretending to type on her keyboard, "is a corporate vice president getting things done! Helping to develop another fifty miles of forest in the Sahara. Laying out a new self-sustaining city in India." She looked down blankly. "I'm not even a hypocrite at this point, because that would imply that I actually *do* something."

The woman's face buckled. Ash couldn't believe it when she saw herself reach out and return the saucer plate to the holder, then affectionately squeeze the top of Naomi's hand.

She said, "But you're all here working on a weekend. Surely..."

"Arbitrary make-work, I promise you. Colors, aesthetics, *trendy* ideas. But if we're building for the long term, won't everything we choose today be considered tacky at some point? No, jobs simply don't have the same kind of meaning that they used to." Naomi sniffled and rubbed her nose.

"This is a new kind of strain," Ash said gently. "Maybe no one was prepared for it. I wish I knew the way forward for you."

Naomi shrugged her shoulders. "I'd say just stay busy, like the nuns used to do. But..."

Ash tried to crack a smile. "We're all too far gone to qualify for that kind of life. Their world doesn't even exist anymore."

"Find her killer, won't you!" A tear trickled down Naomi Blanchard's cheek. "Please?"

Ash felt her chest heave out a great, relieving sigh. "Something to keep me busy at least, right?" she said.

"And maybe to get an answer too. If I just *knew* what the hell happened to her, then maybe..."

"I hear you," Ash said, rising reluctantly. "There's got

to be *a reason* for us to start moving forward again. Instead of..."

Naomi nodded, then simulated rubbing her pubic area.

"Be well, Ashley. Maybe we're not so alone as we think. Goodbye..."

Ash walked out of Larimar Logistics in a daze. She thanked Aphrodite when she passed through the lobby and the eunuch wasn't there to interrupt her reverie by saying something idiotic. Because she was that close to losing all self-control—and would have relished shattering him against one of those pastel blue walls.

But as of yet, there was still no technology available to resuscitate humans in the way that objects could be replaced. Otherwise Mallory Quentin—as well as the friend of her overnight lover Vernon—might both still be alive.

11. ARMS RACE OF CHAOS

Vernon slept very late. He awoke not knowing if it was all a dream. The bite mark on his wrist was living proof—but had that come from Club Dionysus or Ashley?

Ash... Did he really score with that hard-bodied cop? The goddess who looked better than any of the women with exaggerated proportions in his video games? Had he actually made her scream with delight?

Vernon lay in his tiny bed trying to relive it all. He didn't even mind how, later on, she kicked him out of the Express Pod she'd rented a couple miles from where they first met—outside the convenience store where his friend Dayve had died so horribly.

Left to make his own way home—the ride on her ATV apparently being only one-way—Vernon had passed by that terrible place in the haze of early dawn. He couldn't even bring himself to look directly at the spot where Dayve fell.

Poor Dayve! What had happened to him? Just one of the countless boys orphaned in the mad rush that followed that first AI breakthrough some twenty years ago, when entire industries and economic sectors changed almost overnight. From farm workers to construction crews, virtually all blue-collar jobs were replaced by the WFM: Worker-Factory-Mechanic. These sons of the laboring classes were caught in an impossible squeeze—because on the other side, girls were being fast-tracked into higher education and the best careers beyond.

This Moses Generation was shuffled into hastily built dormitories around the country and raised by robot caretakers. While most of the infants did survive, early models of these bots did not understand the subtleties of the human life cycle—and only later were more comprehensive software updates installed.

And so these boys, particularly those orphaned during the first five years, suffered both from malnutrition and emotional deprivation. What prevented their complete retardation was the near-infinite selection of video games available to play on systems that were installed in each dorm room.

Incredible gaming skills and camaraderie developed among them as they learned to rely upon one another while conducting deep space missions, building virtual sports franchises, and recreating the great sailing expeditions of the past.

Vernon had known Dayve for more than ten years. They lived in different dorms on opposite sides of a common courtyard, and had played a number of rounds of *Mongolian Dinosaur Invasion* as teammates before realizing they were neighbors. He met Xaniel not long after.

They had talked about maybe one day taking a trip to other cities that had their own gamer villages. Faraway places like Boston and Las Vegas. But there was never enough money in their monthly stipends to save anything.

Bouts of illness and chronic fatigue also afflicted these boys—and the flu tended to carry a number of them to their graves each year.

Premature death and suicide were common among this outcast group of second-class citizens. They were uneducated, spurned by the beautiful and the functional, and completely ignored by the professions. Seen as a nuisance by a society too humane to euthanize them, Vernon couldn't help but think that the world gave a secret sigh of relief every time a runt died.

The subsequent waves of outcasts had been better cared for. The most beautiful and talented among them were sought after for their prized traits, then formally adopted to serve as fashion models, sex workers, and members of the circus. All that Vernon's own group could hope for was to win gaming prizes, or to receive sexual alms from a member of the elite who was either curious or on a reckless streak.

Because he, like all the rest killing time in the Towers, was too short in stature for the exciting life. *Had been*, at least, until the wee hours of last night. That vicarious thrill he'd almost caught hold of at Club Dionysus— where he was just hoping to go along for the ride, like a flea burrowing into a dog's fur—suddenly it had swallowed him whole and sent him down into the raging storm of Ashley's lust.

He wasn't even sure he *did* much of anything during their encounter. One moment her hands were mashing his face against her taut jutting breasts. Then she heaved him onto the floor and straddled him, her head tilted back toward the ceiling, before leaning down and pressing her lips against his own... licking his face up and down... her teeth nibbling on his earlobe...

Vernon opened his eyes and looked around the dorm room. Still pathetic. Dirty shirts strewn here. Pants tossed into a pile in the corner. Socks and underwear in seemingly every crevice. It would be an embarrassment, if anyone actually cared.

There wasn't as much trash, only because the building's sensors were finely tuned to prevent infestations. Any room that reached a certain threshold of accumulated garbage was subject to instant fumigation. A couple of those invasive tornadoes and you learned just how dirty you could let the place get without setting off any triggers.

Vernon shuffled over to his chair. He reached for the game controller—and saw the bite mark again. It was *for real*. Richly purple, with detailed edges and indents around the two curving arcs.

It had been *for him*. *Because* of him. Proof or a thank-you for a job well done. Not bad for a forgotten son who had so little real-life sexual experience.

But he was learning. To adapt in the moment... when urges tumbled out of control... when steps were leapfrogged... when staggering crescendos were reached. It was an arms race of chaos so much more intense than the orderly fantasy games he played, where you could even simulate sex with a female newscaster while she reported on the events of the day.

Grappling with women in the flesh brought a whole different set of consequences too. The computer vixens only receded so far before eventually giving in—and later they always reached a shuddering climax, because their programmed purpose was to serve you. But how many times had Vernon felt the brutal pang of a real girl drifting away for any number of inscrutable reasons? A wrong word, too aggressive a touch... his not being muscular enough, not strong enough...

Dayve! What had Dayve been saying at the end of the night? That he was feeling weak. Crashing hard. From

that mystery drug! What the hell was it called? It had taken him so high—Vernon had never seen anything like Dayve's exuberant performance out on the dance floor. And where did he get the strength to rip out that cash register?

Probably a side effect of the tasty. You couldn't always expect a smooth flight, or predict when turbulence might careen into an awful crash at the end of a dose.

Experimenting with these nano pills was his group's main pastime besides gaming. And just as no one would dare unplug their computers or shut down the public arcades, a few intoxicated boys out on the town was seen as part and parcel of a world in transition.

But despite their lack of education and opportunity, not all runts were morons. They had been communicating on their gaming headsets for years. Some were even digging into the bigger ideas that lay behind this system which had excluded them.

And so it was that beneath the worldwide clean-up and build-out, beyond the liberation from drudgery and subsequent dawn of decadence... at least one revolution was brewing. This micro-generation of discarded boys, to whom so little was given and nothing expected—they had been plotting. A declaration of relevance. A reclamation of dignity. A plea to participate in the human race.

But they rarely discussed such things. Surveillance was pervasive in this era of super-tech. At most there were whispers, or words spoken in the heat of game play that were actually coded messages alluding to what would happen "one day."

One day. But now Dayve would never see that golden dawn which each runt in his own way envisioned. To stand proudly. To live with hope and be free of the lingering dread they awoke to each morning.

Vernon heard a knock at the door. He nearly jumped

out of his gaming recliner. Who the hell could it be? The guys *always* pinged each other before dropping in—just a common courtesy among those who lived in such cramped quarters and had nowhere else in the world to go or call their own.

He tapped a sequence of buttons to patch the front door security camera feed onto the TV—and froze. His eyes grew wide as the game controller slipped from his fingers onto the carpet.

Detective Ashley Westgard was standing outside in the hall with her arms folded. Vernon thought he might die.

12. JUST LIKE THAT

Security footage from the convention center and hotel took until the late afternoon to fully gather and organize. The investigation team was summoned to the debriefing room shortly after Ash had returned to police headquarters following her interview with Naomi Blanchard.

Chief of Detectives Gabriela Paraquez provided a case summary and updates regarding the murder of Mallory Quentin.

The deceased was an internationally recognized public policy maker and university professor in town to attend the weekend Cheri Chat conference. She had been in good health and had no criminal record.

After giving her speech, Ms. Quentin spent an hour at the hotel bar where witnesses saw her leave with a young woman named Irma Dizon. They retired to Quentin's suite. At some point while Irma was inside the bedroom Clam Bake, Mallory was murdered out in the living room. Irma had since been interviewed and was not considered a suspect.

"Now," Chief Paraquez said, "*someone* slipped into that room, did this nasty business, and then managed to leave the hotel undetected."

"With all that blood?" someone up front asked incredulously. "They couldn't have gone into the bathroom to wash up. Otherwise we'd probably have two victims."

"It would seem so." Paraquez brought a thumb to her chin. "Now, we've finally obtained all the footage from last night. Tech spent the last few hours piecing together what we believe to be the most likely window for our suspect to have come and gone. I've got it synced—all twenty cameras' worth—and I'm gonna run everything at double speed. Keep your eyes open, folks. Bounce around from screen to screen and take notes. Let's see if we can ID our perp within the hour."

Ash had ignored Ted Gillard's invitation to sit next to him in the front row. Now she kicked up a leg onto an empty chair from her seat in the back, and slipped on the pair of zebra-striped aqua spectacles that she wore to make herself seem attentive during these group meetings. Usually she would rather be out pursuing suspects on her ATV, but this case actually mattered to her, so now she paid close attention.

A number of large LCDs, either mounted to the wall or rolled in on TV stands, flashed on and began playing back footage from the previous evening.

The hotel lobby was bustling with a steady stream of patrons—some stopping at the check-in counter before making their way to the elevators; others walked toward the restaurant or pool deck. Elevator cameras showed people blinking, chatting, scratching their heads, and adjusting their bags before exiting on various floors.

The corridors of Mallory Quentin's floor were as busy as would be expected on a Saturday night in a hotel that was hosting a convention.

"There you go," a voice said quietly from somewhere in the darkened debriefing room. "Front wall, middle."

Ash watched Quentin lead young Irma Dizon down the hallway with a firm hand on the back. A classic move. Ash tapped the tip of her index finger against her nostril in silent approval.

A short while later, the sped-up video showed a male member of the hotel staff puttering down the hallway with his head bowed over a food service cart. He paused outside Mallory Quentin's suite door and knocked.

The roomful of police officers now all leaned forward and focused on the screen that showed this critical moment.

The employee, who was wearing a uniform of dress shirt, waistcoat, and slacks, reached into a pocket and pulled out a keycard. But before he could wave it in front of the sensor, the door swung open and the figure of Mallory Quentin wearing a floral kimono came into view. The two appeared to speak briefly, then Quentin stepped aside and the man pushed the cart past her into the suite.

"My god," someone muttered with a whistle. "Just like that."

"Now, now," Chief Paraquez said, "we don't yet know that for sure. Let's keep watching."

A short time later the door opened again. Now a young man in tennis attire with a large gym bag slung over his shoulder stepped out into the hallway.

"What the hell?!" people gasped.

"Who's *that?*"

But Ashley Westgard knew. She had seen a very similar face in the hours following the murder of Mallory Quentin.

She pursed her lips, pulling the stylish glasses down while she considered her options. She decided to wait before saying anything. Better to see what the rest of this watch party revealed. Ash sat back in her seat.

Now the officers began chatting among themselves, trying to help each other work through what they were seeing in order to piece together a plausible narrative.

"Where's he headed?"

"Right onto the *elevator?* Gutsy move."

"What's in that bag?"

"Tennis gear—or the bellhop's getup?"

"*Tennis gear?* Are you serious?"

"Hey, we don't know who he was. Maybe a guest of the victim politely leaving her alone for some romance."

"To play tennis at nine o'clock?"

"Knock it off, will ya? Keep watching!"

"Thank you."

Some mild laughter made its way around the room.

The elevator doors opened and everyone turned their eyes toward the screen which showed the lobby. The man in white shorts made a beeline not toward the sports complex as expected, but directly through the front sliding doors into the loading area. Now glances shifted to this outside view. The man got into a driverless cab and was on his way.

"Now *that* takes mammaries!" someone marveled.

"And then he was gone."

The videos all paused. Paraquez said, "All right, that's a good start. Let's watch it through again. Look for other details this time. And keep spitballing."

The following connections were made during the second viewing:

-Suspect was seen entering the hotel lobby half an hour before the time of Mallory Quentin's murder. He was carrying the gym bag and wearing the same skimpy white shorts and collared shirt.

-Partial views showed him entering a supply closet on

the floor below the crime scene. A few minutes later he exited this closet wearing the bellhop's outfit and rode the elevator down to the kitchen. Shortly he returned to the supply closet rolling the service cart, which was laden with a champagne bucket and stainless-steel covered plate. His actions were obscured momentarily, then he took the elevator to Quentin's floor.

Now the assembled officers were silent, each grinding gears in their heads.

"Well, you can see his face right there!" someone said. "What about a scan?"

"Nothing came up," Paraquez said. "Maybe false contacts? We don't know yet. But *something* threw off the face match."

"Fucking smooth, this guy," a voice marveled.

"Yeah," another said, "but how did he just waltz into the kitchen to get that booze and food?"

"Especially if no one on the staff ever saw him before. Which we think is correct?"

"Someone must've ordered it all beforehand."

"The victim—or someone *else?*"

Chief Paraquez flipped up the light dimmers. "Now you're cookin'," she said. "We've got some new leads to pursue, yes indeed. Such as where'd that cab drop him off? And assuming the murder weapon and bloody clothes were in the gym bag, where is it now? What else?"

"Did he scope out the hotel? Or did an accomplice do that for him?"

"As part of a hit team? Mother of God, I hope not," Paraquez said. "Come on, gimme more."

"How did he know for sure that the victim was in her room? What, was he just gonna stand out there all night?"

"He had a key, remember?" Ash said.

"Ah..."

"And," she continued, "it looked like he was planning to let himself in and wait for Ms. Quentin to return whenever. That girl Irma doesn't know how lucky she is. Nine times out of ten, he kills them both."

"Right, right," Paraquez said. "This is why you guys do what you do—you're good cops! I need five minutes to assign teams to fan out over parts of the hotel we may have overlooked. And tech's gonna have to pull footage from the city tracking the route that cab took. Any questions?"

As the group separated to head out on their new assignments, Ash waited for Ted to leave the room before brushing up against Chief Paraquez.

"Say, boss," she said. "I might know who your killer is."

Paraquez looked up from her tablet, expression unchanged. "Yeah? Talk to me."

"It's just a hunch right now. So I don't want to say anything. Can you give me a little time to inquire... in my own way?"

"I'm surprised at you, Detective Westgard. This isn't like you at all. In fact, your fists are usually flying by now. What gives?"

Ash put her glasses into a hard shell case. "Something about all this just doesn't sit right with me. There's more going on here. I think the others were right when they said someone else might be involved."

"Who do you think?" Paraquez asked.

"That, I don't know. But give me a chance to feel it out, yeah?"

Paraquez exhaled. "This is *bad*. For public safety, not to mention tourism. And Quentin was a heavyweight. This could be national news. We need to solve this thing quick! So go on, Ash. Do what it takes to bring him in."

Westgard nodded. "Of that I can guarantee you."

13. ROLLER COASTER

She couldn't believe she was doing this. Or that she *had* to do it this way. But there was potentially too much at stake to sit back and wait for the data to break the case— as so often happened in an era when computers making light-speed connections could button up crimes by themselves.

It wasn't the extra effort that bothered her either. Nor was she scared by the prospect of having to face down one of her conquests. Murder was at play now. A big fish, too. Not just some local street urchin who probably had it coming. Allowing the case to languish while relying on the bots wasn't a good look for the police department. Conversely, whoever brought in the collar would get the commendations, the honors, and perhaps a promotion...

Detective Ashley Westgard *knew* that they would get their man. She just had to manage it in a certain way, because... Well, even that was more complicated than she wanted to acknowledge.

First, if the murderer did have an accomplice, then the case contained an unknown layer beyond what she and only she was privy to. There was also something that Naomi Blanchard had said which left Ash holding a curious thread. It suggested that there might be an even bigger context to the story, as if dark clouds were crawling in over the whole world.

Finally, on top of everything, there was Vernon. The runt who had knocked her mind right out of the park. Got those million fingers pulsing across the surface of her brain like a piano maestro tickling the keys. Her first orgasm in nearly a year.

She had rewarded him kindly. First, a full swallow. Then she sank a deep bite into the side of his wrist. Her *real* autograph.

So she'd felt no hesitation about giving him the boot after they'd passed out in that rental pod for a while. *Good work, kid. Fluid exchange completed. See ya never.*

Or so she thought. Because the face that had revealed itself on the Elixir Hotel security footage belonged to the young man who spent the night sprawled out on a sidewalk, his torn body hidden underneath a sheet.

Ash had given this dead would-be thief a quick look while on her way back inside the convenience store, just before she set her own sexual plot into motion. The half of his face that remained clearly resembled that of the hotel killer—but as of yet, the police department's computers still hadn't made the connection. So much for relying on the bots!

After a brief discussion with Officers Blaine and Cantwell by the front counter, Ash had gone back outside and commanded the boring Xaniel to go home. Once she was finally alone with Vernon, she put her boot up on the ambulance's fender and laid out her offer as plain as day: Lady Lust was inviting him to join her for the full Club Dionysus experience.

Now as she strutted through the entrance of Tower

S-3, Ash felt the awestruck stares of the young runts hanging out in the lobby. Let them ogle—she would absorb their longing like Vitamin D.

Still, this little dopamine rush wasn't enough to chase away the shade of... that new apprehension she felt darting around her mind, and which was getting more complicated by the day. What *was* it?

This Vernon... Friend of the perp who had committed a savage murder, gone out on the town afterward, and then inexplicably jeopardized his clean getaway by holding up a convenience store. Something didn't fit. Were Vernon and Xaniel somehow involved after all? Ash had dealt with enough criminals and liars in her day to find it hard to believe that these two other runts were play-acting. Their grief for Dayve and shock about the robbery seemed genuine.

Or was she getting it all confused by the fact that she had not only slept with Vernon, but he'd successfully gotten her off? And now, forced by circumstance to see him again so soon...

Sure, she'd played with a few sexy hooligans in her day, but this time it felt like Vernon was one up on the scoreboard. As if he had something on her.

That was it. Ashley Westgard *did not* like situations where she was not in full control. And right now she felt... Vulnerable was too strong of a word. *Dangerously human* was more like it—and that made her nervous enough. Because the bad decisions made while feeling doubtful always left an aftertaste worse than those jumped into head first.

She knew that her mind was spiraling into crazy town, but couldn't do a damn thing about it. One particular voice kept suggesting that she should probably let Vernon knock her up. And then what? Chase after suspects with a distended belly? Install a child seat onto the back of her

ATV? Ludicrous! Did runts even produce sperm? She couldn't keep track of which groups got snipped or sterilized...

And besides, who actually *had babies* nowadays? Leave that to the labs! All those cute little incubators, lined up in neat rows and set to the perfect brewing temperature. Where there was no risk of toxins. The child's features would be pre-selected. *And*, you didn't ruin your breasts feeding and pumping...

Ash looked down at her own rack, then tugged her jacket zipper open. She wanted to smack Vernon silly with the sight of her tits fighting against the sparkling confines of her bra. To even the score and reestablish herself as the dominant one.

Still, he *had* squeezed and chomped on those puppies like a wild forest animal in the blue neon glow of that Express Pod...

Vernon snapped out of his double take. Instinctively he dashed around the little room and picked up all the bits of mess. He threw socks, cups, trash, anything and everything into the bathroom and shut the door. Let the bots show what they were worth as they sorted, disposed, cleaned, and folded it all.

He looked around. It was so dark. He turned up the dimmers. But what about himself? Quickly he slid open the bathroom door, hoping the bots hadn't yet been summoned by the sanitation sensors. Yes, the mess was still there on the floor.

Another knock at the door. *Shit!* Vernon quickly wetted his hair, combed it out. The blond strands tapered down nicely over his forehead. Next he grabbed a bottle of cologne—Highland King—and sprayed it under his arms and onto his neck.

He closed up the bathroom again and went to the front

door. He took a deep shuddering breath. *She* was only three feet away!

"You sure do make a girl wait," Ash said to him after he'd slowly pulled the door open. She was gnawing on gum with big exaggerated chews. It smelled good—zesty peppermint. *Damn!* He'd forgotten to take a swig of mouthwash.

"Hey," Vernon said as casually as his throbbing heart could muster. "A man in his castle, you know. Say, you got any more of that gum?"

"Sure," she said, dipping two fingers into the space between her breasts. "Can I come in?"

"Okay."

She gave him the plastic tube, closing the door behind herself as she stepped inside. Vernon popped a piece into his mouth, snapped the top shut, and—instead of handing the container back as he would have done any other day of his life—he reached out and stuffed it back down into her bra. He even gave it an extra push with the tip of his finger.

Maybe it was the cologne. Or some ancient line of code in his DNA that had activated. Because the gods seemed to be manning the joystick of his life right now. He felt his mind floating in a dizzy mix of nerves and excitement.

Ash surveyed the cramped room. It was dominated by the giant TV screen and gaudy gaming recliner that sat in the middle like a throne. Small tables, cup holders, game accessories, and wet wipe dispensers were arrayed within strategic arm's reach of the chair. Two saggy bean bag chairs were over by the window. And the unmade twin bed, which occupied a dark corner, was much too small of a mat for the kind of gymnastics that she engaged in.

"Nice place you got here," she said. "Cozy."

"Did you come by to play games... or fuck?" Vernon

was shocked to hear himself even say these words, let alone with such baritone gusto.

"Ha!" Ash snorted, but not too harshly. "Listen to you. I knew you were cute... but funny, too? 'Hello, Dad? I think I met the one!' "

Vernon sensed that the muscles on his face might start quivering if she kept hitting him with these little barbs. Already he felt his confidence—or was it just the adrenaline?—draining away.

"Um," he said hesitantly, "I didn't think you ever wanted to see me again."

Ash flashed her teeth. The mangled little piece of gum was trapped between them helplessly. "You're right," she said. "I didn't. But... you were crying in your sleep last night. I thought I'd better check in and see how you were holding up. Watching a friend die like that must have been very traumatic."

Vernon wished that whoever was holding the game controller would press the code that warped him out of danger back to the mothership. He didn't have the strength to battle this creature for long. He was just a runt. His kind only knew what to do with scraps or the occasional joyride. But facing a real woman one on one? In the middle of the day when they were both sober? This was far different from those midnight confessionals, where runts were nothing more than outlets for upper-class women's secret perversions.

He turned away to hide his fearful shame. If he had truly done what she said—wept in that bed, in her arms—was it really for Dayve? Or for himself? Or in overwhelmed gratitude for the fragment of distilled joy that life had at last bestowed upon him, however fleetingly? Or worse, did he weep because such affairs were as forgettable as a morning meal to the gilded members of society?

He *wanted* to cry now, thinking it might have been better to never know that pleasure at all. Because it had revealed to him the cost—that what meant everything to him was dead skin to the likes of Ashley Westgard. A terrible new dread was burrowing down into his heart as a result.

"Dayve's not the first friend of mine to die," Vernon said finally, turning toward her with a fierceness that masked the weight of his grief. "I've said goodbye plenty of times. We get together and watch the urn go down the chute. Runts are the only family they ever had."

Ash sensed that she had cut him down low enough. She decided to relent. "I'm sorry," she said softly. "You did well last night, Bull Rider." She offered a smile. "Thank you."

Vernon felt himself rejuvenated, like a torrent of air bubbles escaping the ocean floor and surging toward the surface. He leaned back against the wall. He didn't trust his jelly legs to support him through the next turn on this roller coaster ride.

He saw her approach slowly, put a hand on his chest. Lean in and kiss him. Lips glossy. Tongue probing—*stealing* the gum from his mouth!

She eased back, grinning. Then gave a deep sigh. "Now, Mister Vernon," she said, "here's the deal. Brace yourself. It's about to get real heavy."

He nodded. "I'm ready."

"Do you know who Mallory Quentin is?"

"No."

"Ever heard of something called Cheri Chat?"

"Mm-mm."

Ash turned on her heel and began to pace slowly back and forth in front of him.

"The thing is," she said, "your friend Dayve did. Very well, in fact."

"He never mentioned anything about it to me."

A pause. "I'm glad to hear that. Vernon... have you checked the news today?"

"No, I've been too..." He almost smiled, then checked himself. "I don't really keep up with all that."

"Right," Ash said. "Well, if you had, you'd know that last night Ms. Quentin was brutally murdered in her suite at the Elixir Hotel."

Vernon's eyes tracked Ash on her slow sentry's march across the room.

"And I," she said, "have reason to believe—in fact, I *know*—that Dayve was inside the hotel at the time of her killing."

"What?" Vernon stepped off the wall. "But you know I was with him last night."

"The *entire* evening?"

"I mean, we all met up at the arcade."

"What time? This is very important."

Vernon thought for a moment. "Like, ten or eleven?"

Ash poked him in the nipple. "Thank you very much for that confirmation." She licked across the surface of her top lip.

"Of what? Why?"

"That helps us both. And it means you're in the clear, pal."

"Wait," Vernon said. "Was I... a suspect?"

"Well, you weren't *not* one until now. You see," Ash said, tapping a finger into the palm of her other hand, "Ms. Quentin was killed at approximately eight forty-five. Thus giving your friend plenty of time to flee the scene, dispose of the evidence, and jump back into the swing of a fun Saturday night as if nothing had ever happened."

Vernon's head was spinning. "That's insane! Impossible! I still don't understand what made him snap outside the store. Because there, he was saying something about being weak, not going back...”

“What do you think he meant?”

“The tasties... It's just...” Vernon brought his hand up, wiping away a sudden tear from each eye with thumb and forefinger. “You won't understand. You just can't...”

“Tell me. Please, try.” Ash couldn't believe how compassionate her voice sounded. Was it just a ploy to get information, or did she actually care?

“We all know what we are,” Vernon said, softly but with determination. “Little shits. Stains the world doesn't know what to do with. But the pills... Once you get that nano crawling through you... You feel alive! Then later, when you realize the ride's ending... It sucks. I know some guys who stopped taking any of it. They'd rather live flat than have to come back down into the mud. I'll try, for like a week. But then the traders show up with some new boost...”

“And Dayve?” Ash said.

“Maybe he hit terminal velocity.”

“Ah.”

She knew the expression. Street slang for when users passed some internal breaking point and their bodies or spirit refused to return to sobriety—to limits. They would pop or drink or *do* anything to extend the rush. Steal from relatives, lick battery acid, whatever it took to keep acquiring and ramping up higher and higher. Eventually they all *physically* crashed in one way or another. Falls, fights, suicides, arrests... and shootings.

“What do you think might have pushed your friend over the edge?” Ash asked.

“That's what I don't get,” Vernon said. “We had a great night out! But... he was on something new.”

“A pill?”

“Yeah. He didn't even know what it was called.”

"Where'd he get it?" Ash moved closer to Vernon.

"Uh..." he said. "A guy his normal seller brought along."

"When?" Ash was alert now.

"Earlier in the day sometime. Late afternoon or evening, maybe?"

"Where? And be specific."

"That, I don't know."

Ash cast out her arm. "What, you didn't ever buy that stuff together?"

"I mean..." Vernon paused. "It's kind of personal. You find a good thing, a supplier you can trust... You get possessive. I mean yeah, we share the nano itself, but never the connect."

"Shit!" Ash rasped. Her mind was racing now. She'd have to pull the video following Dayve around for the whole day possibly. "Okay, let's not get ahead of ourselves. Did Dayve live in this dorm?"

"No. But it's just across the way."

"Come on, then. Put on your shoes. We're going over there."

Vernon looked down. He had been talking to her this whole time in sock feet. The Highland King was mortified.

They rode the elevator down in silence. Vernon felt his confidence slowly return as he sensed the other orphans watching them out in the courtyard. He tried to match this statuesque cop-goddess's lengthy step stride for stride. He puffed out his chest, keeping his gaze straight ahead, leading—yes, leading the way for this woman who had used him, discarded him unceremoniously, and then suddenly come back.

He showed Ash where Dayve's room was. She briefly inspected the door lock, then pulled out her phone and tapped around the screen for a minute. There was a click.

"That easy?" Vernon said.

"Yep. I didn't *have* to knock."

Ash gave him a wink and then pushed the apartment door open. Another mess. These gamer types certainly were a disheveled bunch. Nature or lack of nurture? At least Vernon had made some sort of effort to clean up while she waited in the hall. A knock on *his* door for both their sakes.

"Oh my god!" she said.

"What?" Vernon said, walking in behind her.

"I can't believe it."

She sprang forward, then knelt down next to Dayve's gaming recliner. There on the carpet was the same gym bag she had seen in the hotel surveillance footage.

"Don't touch *anything*," she said almost viciously. Then, more softly, "For your protection. I promise you."

Vernon hated himself for allowing his heart to be tossed by the waves of Ashley Westgard's flicking tongue. This Earth Mother who in one moment offered limitless hope—a glorious horizon that would inspire him to perform any heroic deed she might require—before hurtling him into the hollow despair of her disdain. The goddess had chosen another! Or perhaps no one at all. What mattered was that the lovely warmth of her gaze no longer shone upon you.

"Whatever you say," he whispered sadly.

"He *did it*, Vernon," she hissed. "He killed her!"

Vernon dropped his head, knowing that the worst moment of his desperate little life had arrived. A torrent of tears came down and his body quivered pathetically in the presence of his queen. Nothing had ever prepared him for this awful collision of emotion, yearning, and pain. That the doorway to connecting with another human soul, which should have infused him with power, instead reduced him to mush dripping down onto the floor...

"My goodness," Ash said, moving very close to him. "What's happened to you?"

She seemed to observe herself from afar: Hands rubbing his upper arms. Lifting his face by the cheeks and watching the tears gush down between her fingers. Almost losing herself in that moment. Then throwing her arms around his body, pulling him into her, the thick warmth of her chest and arms and back, completely absorbing him and nearly crushing his little frame.

"Why?" Vernon was crying. "What is this all about?"

"I wish I knew," she said, burying her face into his hair.

"I don't think I can go on... I can't *take* it!" he howled.

Ash pulled back, still holding his arms. "But Vernon, you have to bear it. I *need* you to help me."

"What? How can I... ?"

"Because," she said, opening her stance and pointing to the gym bag, "Dayve didn't do this all by himself. Someone put your friend up to killing Mallory Quentin and I want to know why. Don't you?"

Vernon's chest heaved. "I don't know anything anymore."

Ash chuckled and gave him a tender smile. She touched his cheek.

"Welcome to real life, babe," she said. "You just graduated from the gamer's chair."

"I did?"

Vernon felt himself ramping up yet again. Ashley Westgard, the ultimate drug he'd ever tasted, held out her hand to him once more. She was going to take him into the world.

"Now let's go," Ash said. "We've got work to do."

He couldn't say no.

14. HER MELON SCENT

Vernon could feel the phone vibrating in his thigh pocket. It was Xaniel trying to reach him for the tenth time today. He hadn't had the heart to face him after last night's agonizing experience at the convenience store. So much else had happened—and was now happening—that Vernon justified leaving his friend to languish alone because he needed to stay in the moment.

The wind whipped against the sides of his arms. His face was shielded by Ashley's body and helmet as they raced along the Jacksonville streets. He sat forward in the seat and wrapped his arms around her waist tenderly, losing himself in her melon scent as he nuzzled his face into her back.

There was no extra helmet for him to wear, but he wasn't concerned. If the ATV crashed and he split his skull open and died, it would be with a fullness in his heart so foreign and wonderful that it was almost unbearable.

As his queen slowed the vehicle before turning into the police station parking lot, Vernon tried to blink away the puffiness that was returning to his eyes. He really would have to get a grip on himself if he had any expectation of keeping this Amazon cop around.

He jumped off, then stood aside while Ash fiddled with the ATV's console. She tapped the handgun holstered on her hip before removing her helmet.

"More gum?" she said, offering several pieces in the palm of her leather glove.

He took one, adding as he dropped it into his mouth, "I'm keeping this, too."

"Oh yeah? Your loss." She smirked and gave a wave. "Come on."

They had to stand aside briefly before entering the building. A bulbous gray repair-bot was welding a seam beside the door, and sparks were falling onto the ground.

"Pardon me," the bot said in a watery voice. It disabled the tool. "Another day, another dollar..."

Vernon followed Ash into the station lobby. An elderly couple was peering at a holographic display on the left side wall. A long graphite bench ran down the right side of the room. On it sat a middle-aged man holding a car side mirror in his lap, a set of triplet schoolgirls wearing matching gingham dresses, and a college-aged redhead with a briefcase between her feet.

"Officers..."

Ash gave a casual wave to the fifty-something policewoman and obelisk-shaped bot that were behind the reception desk.

A door that could be activated by several triggers—employee badge, facial and retinal scans, or fingerprint—slid open and they entered the core of the police station. Vernon saw several cops swiping away at workstations with large square touchscreens. Others holding coffees were chatting around a long table that was filled with rumpled periodicals.

"Take a seat," Ash said to him curtly. "Be right back."

He watched her sidle up to the assembled group—four women and a man. They all exchanged playful jabs with her, then leaned in to hear what she had to say. When they drew back and guffawed, Vernon regretted having let her convince him to come here.

Was she making fun of him right now? Telling them about the size of his penis? He didn't understand all the cues that passed between members of the upper classes when they were in their own element.

But living where he did, Vernon knew that law enforcement was dangerous enough for them to be much more grounded than the real dandies. Like those arrogant lesbians who had yelled at him and his friends on the sidewalk last night. *They* didn't have to do anything, unlike cops who actually put their lives on the line.

Vernon had been around plenty of police activity during his life. Whether the Towers were originally built in places of neglect, or if crime and all its detritus had gravitated there over the years—the fact was that what the runts called home could be a very scary place at times. It was another reason that he and many of the other orphans mostly stayed indoors. Because if they were already at a disadvantage against the functional members of above-board society, then they were simply no match for the rejects who prowled the streets in search of weaker prey.

And despite a surveillance network that boasted millions of interconnected sensors, if the police came around to the Towers it usually meant that the crime had already taken place. They were just there to order up the ambulance for a runt whose eye socket had been shattered in an unprovoked assault. To go through the formalities of filling out a missing person report on someone who had been snatched and would likely never be found. Or to send a lifeless body down to the morgue.

Which is why Vernon had been shocked to see so much active interest in a runt-related case this time. His own personal involvement with Ash notwithstanding, there was something about the Dayve situation that animated her differently from what he was used to seeing when it came to life and death in the Towers.

Even that was puzzling, because every so often a runt snapped and didn't just take it out on himself. Vernon remembered the sensational story from two years ago when a guy named Neal had tried to kill a stranger. The kid had learned how to lasso from some Wild West video game, then went down to a fancy shopping district and caught a gorgeous young woman in a mini-skirt by the leg with his rope. He dragged her into the street hoping a car would come along and run her over.

But a place like Zuma Drive, with all its jewelry and celebrity fashion stores, left no crevice unmonitored, and within seconds of the woman's first screams a two-bot security team had descended upon the attacker. They whipped out hoses and sprayed a fast-expanding gooey foam that immobilized him.

The intended victim only suffered a few scrapes on her hands and knees, which any of the nearby salons would have been able to zap away. Everyone else left this episode feeling a little more disdain for runts.

Neal had been tried for attempted murder and subsequently deported to his ancestral homeland of Wales. Under normal circumstances offenders worked their way up the punishment hierarchy—which included community service and local lockup—but this offense was deemed sufficient cause for remedial repatriation.

Vernon never did get any updates about how well Neal, the would-be rustler, was getting on among his own people.

Dayve's case seemed to be a different matter entirely. His death *and* the other death which Ash was laying at his doorstep. Not that Vernon could actually believe it. *Murder*. How could Dayve perform that mating dance for the lady in the sequin dress at Club Dionysus, if he had really slit the throat of another woman just hours earlier?

"Wake up, Vern. Hey!"

Fingers snapped in his face. He looked up. Ash was standing right in front of him. He heard laughter and saw the other officers shaking their heads.

"Come on," she said. "Time to spill the beans."

"Huh?" he said as he stood up. "I didn't do anything."

"You know what I mean. You're gonna help us fill in a lot of gaps."

Detective Ashley Westgard was liking this. The murder of Mallory Quentin, which had piqued her interest from the start, was now sprouting into something much more significant. If she did this right, a lot of doors might open for her. Maybe even take her life up a notch or two. Beyond the cops who spent their lives dealing with dysfunctional people. Beyond the Naomi Blanchards of the world, whose range of motion was limited to air-conditioned walls. And it would be *earned* through courage and her individual efforts.

Blue collar meets white collar meets... no computer. Because there were still some things that only a human could do, no matter how fast the mainframe processed data or how many pounds of torque the hydraulic arm exerted.

Ash had every right to be nervous with so much at stake. But she held a card that no one else even knew existed. *And* she carried that newfound mental calm thanks to this runt Vernon, who was now sheepishly following her into Chief Paraquez's private office. It was time to earn her stripes.

"Alright, Detective Westgard. Lay it out for me."

Gabriela Paraquez was a no-nonsense law enforcement administrator. Naturally tan, black hair pulled back, modest silver ball-stud earrings. She could have been a spokesmodel for some island resort, had her father and uncle not also both been cops. Action and grit were in her blood.

Ash was seated next to Vernon in front of Paraquez's desk. She said, "As promised, I found our killer."

Gabriela nodded at Vernon. "Is he it?"

"No, ma'am. We'll get to him shortly. But before I dig in, what'd we learn from the footage of that cab our killer took away from the hotel?"

Paraquez tapped her computer screen. "Ahh..." she sighed. "Smart, this one. We tracked it over to the performing arts center, but our perp bailed in a mess of traffic. We lost him in the crush of patrons getting out of the other cabs."

"Come on," Ash said, "don't tell me any of *them* were wearing tennis whites to attend a play?!"

"Our friend threw some regular clothes over that stuff while he was in the back seat. Tech finally received a copy of the in-car footage from the cab company less than an hour ago. So until you walked in here, we had no idea where the suspect was."

"Well, you can call off the search." Ash inspected her sparkling teal fingernails.

Gabriela thumped her fist against the desktop. "That's my lady! Tell me more."

Ash couldn't sit still any longer. She got up and said, "You know that botched smash-and-grab you had me check out?"

"Of course. Easy mop-up for you, no doubt."

Ash felt herself wince for Vernon. She said, "I'll

assume you've ID'd the perp by now—prints, DNA, whatever. But has anyone swung by his place of residence?"

"Oh, not yet," Paraquez said with a wave. "Busy day. He's dead. An orphan, you know how it is..."

"*Chief*," Ash said as she saw Vernon drop his head into his hands, "they are one in the same."

She quickly ran down the overlapping details of the previous night's events, then placed her hands on Vernon's shoulders from behind.

"And that's why I brought this young man to see you. Not only was Vernon there at the time of Dayve's death, he might possess some information that can help us make sense of the Quentin murder."

"I see." Paraquez looked at Vernon and said softly, "I'm sorry about your friend dying. Even if he was... a cold-blooded killer."

Ash silently cursed herself. She knew better than to set her boss up like that. The chief could draw a person in with her beautiful black eyes, then verbally eviscerate them with deadpan razors. Ash readied herself to prop Vernon up, otherwise her whole plan might fall apart.

Vernon shook his head, then spoke for the first time. "He's not a murderer. I knew Dayve for like ten years. He was the same as me, or any of us."

"That may be the case," Paraquez said, "but crime around the Towers is a serious problem. I'm sure you know that. Maybe your friend was mixed up in something you weren't aware of."

"Like what?"

"Oh, I don't know. Theft. Blackmail. Or perhaps he got jilted by a woman who was out of his league, and so he took revenge..."

When Ash saw Paraquez's lips curl into a cruel smile, she decided to jump in before her big moment completely imploded.

"Chief," she said, "here's what we gotta focus on. Whatever tasty Dayve bought earlier in the day, I think *that* is what pushed him over the edge to kill."

Paraquez leaned back. "Okay, I'm listening. So... what exactly? The high alternated from a meticulously calculated kill, to wild partying, to derangement? Forgive me if I don't buy it—something's missing here."

"I know! The *how* and the *why*. And it all leads to another *who*. Who sold him that pill?"

"Wait, hold up! Are you suggesting that the pill *remote controlled* Dayve to orchestrate the Quentin killing, and then later caused him to self-destruct?"

"Exactly! To silence him forever."

"But you can't actually believe this!" Now Gabriela was also standing. "The nano inside those drugs simulates any number of feelings and experiences, of course. But to orchestrate a full-on tactical mission? I just don't know if it's possible."

"Look, we aren't scientists," Ash said. "We don't know what they can cook up in the lab. But the way this played out makes me think, not only was the Quentin killing not a random attack, maybe there's more to it than a personal grudge. And that means Dayve was just the intermediary for someone else!"

"Detective Westgard, are you grasping here? Because if you personally found the killer, I would say just take a bow and quit while you're ahead."

"I can't. Forget about this one guy Dayve. *Most people* aren't capable of pulling off what he did at the Elixir. He was calm, cool, meticulous... fucking flawless."

"In theory, you're right. But he *was* a gamer. How many hundreds of virtual spy missions and war games did he role play in over the years?"

"Probably as many as you think. But Chief, I really

think it would be a mistake to ignore the possibility that some mastermind was pulling his strings."

Paraquez sat down again. She said, "That's quite a leap beyond our general suspicion that Dayve may have had an accomplice. So before we start hacking through those weeds, does *he* have anything more to say?"

Vernon glanced at Ash, then said, "I just can't see how Dayve was driven to do this. I mean, life... We're not bad people! If you won't do it for me, can you just find out what happened because it's the truth?"

"*The truth?* Lilith help us." Paraquez motioned around the room. "You see all this, Vernon? It's really real! Not some game where the dead bodies disappear and everything stops when you turn off the TV. In here, the mission never ends. And the truth isn't always nice and neat."

"Okay, Chief," Ash said. "We don't have to rub his nose in it."

Paraquez tapped a finger against the desk three times. She said with finality, "We're gonna pin this on Dayve for now. Tell everyone we found Ms. Quentin's killer—if not the actual motive yet—and maybe we can avoid a scandal here in town. Help me do that, and I'll consider letting you dig deeper. Sound fair?"

"Deal," Ash said. "Now let's head over to the Towers. There's a gym bag we need to book into evidence."

As she followed Vernon out of the office, Ash heard the chief say behind her, "Detective Westgard? That's some solid work you did."

She smiled and flexed her abs.

15. TASTY TRADER

Ash saw his head bobbing between two of the four-foot-diameter pipes that fed into Jacksonville's waste repurposing plants. She clicked her small flashlight on and off from the tree she was standing behind, then trotted out and vaulted the first enormous pipe.

"Hey, chica."

"Eduardo," she replied.

"A surprise to hear from you on a Sunday night. Not that I mind, of course. You need something to help you chill? Or are you making this a long weekend?"

The man was wearing a synthetic woven jacket. Stab-resistant and equipped with a dozen zip pockets, it was the multi-purpose uniform of choice among tasty traders.

Ash chuckled, rubbing her hands together softly. "Maybe. But first I have a few questions for you."

"Ah, Christ," Eduardo said, spitting to his left. "Thought I was gonna make a nice sale to you."

"We'll see." Ash smiled in the faint light. A low hum could be felt and heard coming through the pipes as the city's accumulated refuse pumped along. She said, "You hear of anyone slinging something new and hot?"

"Come on, Mrs. Police. You know we always mix it up. Gotta keep the people interested—or disinterested, hehehe. That's how we stay in business. And relevant. The novelty of our product."

"Okay, well I'm looking for something particular that's making the rounds right now. It might be more than just a new feeling. I'm talking about a drug that could drive a person to kill."

Eduardo threw out his hands innocently. He said, "These things happen. We all know what *enhanced emotions* can lead to. Love, hate, passion, pain! So if you wanna shut us down just because somebody pulls a trigger with tasties in their blood... Well, either the world gets fucking boring real quick—or you create a lot more problems for yourself."

"No one's talking about closing anyone down here," Ash said. "And I *don't* mean incidental contact, either. I think this pill, a big gumball, it was designed to override the nervous system, then direct the user to take someone out."

Eduardo stepped back, saying cautiously, "Hey now. I know the rules. We all do. I don't mess with no nano that's got claws. Only tasties I sell are straight up. Absorb, release, dissolve. Then out with your poop and piss. That's it, I swear!"

"I trust you. I believe you. I really do. But maybe you've heard something? Or seen some new guys on your turf?"

"Man, I don't know. People are always comin' and goin'..."

Ash stepped in close, almost forcing him against the pipe. Then she smiled and backed off.

"Eddie, come on. I'm not here to breathe down your neck. I value our business relationship. But I've got a body in the morgue that was sliced up by a guy who bought from someone in your circle. I just need to find out who that is. Then we can all get back to our regular lives."

Eduardo looked down, exhaling slowly. "Okay," he said. "We know who's who in the game. Got to protect our interests every which way, right? So a dude I know named Clarkus, he been meeting up with a new guy he say is a friend from out of town. Also a trader, wants to learn how we do business down here."

"Now you're making me happy," Ash said. She paused. "How can you let me know where I might bump into this Clarkus fellow—in a way that won't trip you up, of course?"

There was the sound of a zipper opening. Eduardo's hand slid in, then came out holding a round plastic case.

"Make it worth my while?" he said.

"Fair enough. You got anything, uh, new of your own?"

Another pocket was relieved of its contents.

"Oh, lady, lady," he crooned. "I have been saving something very nice, just for you..."

"Yeah? It won't make me kill anyone, right?"

The man laughed. "No way, girl! It'll put you in charge of things—if you can handle it, hehe."

"Hmm. I like the sound of that."

Ash reached into her own pocket, then flicked two fingers forward. Eduardo's hand darted out and snatched the plastic card that was between them.

She grinned in the darkness.

"I always do my best work... *on top*."

16. SCORE ONE FOR THE RUNTS

Vernon knew what *this* knock at the door meant. It filled him with a different kind of dread than before. He had been avoiding Xaniel all day, but now he was cornered and had no choice but to face his friend. He opened the door.

Xaniel was ashen. He said, "Where the hell have you been?"

Vernon closed the door after Xaniel entered the room, then said, "I'm sorry. So much has happened, I—"

"What else could have happened?!" Xaniel nearly yelled. "I was right there with you. And I've been feeling like shit by myself because I couldn't reach you. So spit it out, man."

"Settle down first, Xan. Come on, you want a drink?"

Xaniel went to the center of the room and sat in the gaming recliner. It was an unwritten rule never to claim another runt's main chair without permission, but today Vernon chose not to say anything.

"Gimme something green," Xaniel said.

Vernon walked to the corner of the dorm that served

as his kitchen. Its main feature was an enormous refrigerator set into the wall, which was actually seventy-five-percent freezer and stocked with meals he heated up in the blinkwave oven. This was the ideal setup for gamers who didn't want to waste time cooking, when it could otherwise be spent in the virtual world online.

He opened the smaller fridge door. These shelves were mostly empty, with only a dozen bottles of Lectrolade left. Soon the appliance's internal sensors would order fresh cases to be delivered outside his door. Loading these food and drink supplies was the only manual labor that many runts actually did—and this simply because they didn't like bots entering their units.

Vernon walked to the recliner. He handed Xaniel a bottle of Gaelic Geyser, then twisted open the cap of his own orange Pompeii Potpourri.

"You wanna play something?" Xaniel asked.

"Are you serious?" Vernon said. "Turn on the TV and log on to the network like everything's back to normal?"

Xaniel looked away. "I don't know. Where were you, Vern? I had a rough fucking day. And just now, I went past Dayve's room. There are cops everywhere! That never happens when we get fragged. Or go batshit."

Vernon compressed his lips, unsure of how to start dumping the rest of the story onto Xaniel's lap. He held out his wrist so that Ash's bite mark showed.

"See that?" he said. "I got it last night."

"At the club?" Xaniel said.

"No. Later. After you left."

"Wait, that fucking cop took you home?! I *thought* she was sizing you up."

"Well, not home. But I got her."

Xaniel jumped up from the chair and threw his arms around Vernon. "Yeah! Score one for the runts!" He pulled back. "But what does that have to do with...

anything?"

Suddenly Vernon lost his composure and blurted it all out in a torrent.

"You wanna know why everyone is crawling around Dayve's place? Because he fucking killed some important woman at a hotel before we even went to the arcade! And the cop lady thinks that whatever new tasty he took made him do it!"

As tears once again overcame him, Vernon turned away and leaned against the wall. But Xaniel followed him and demanded, "How do you know all this? For the last time, where've you been all day?"

"That cop, Ash. She was at the other murder scene first. They sent her to us by chance—and then later she saw Dayve on the hotel security footage."

"Oh my god... This is gonna come back to bite us all."

"What do you mean?" Vernon turned to look at his friend.

Xaniel said, "Picture the headlines. 'Another Runt Loses His Mind.' 'The Gamer Killer—When is Enough Enough?' "

"And then what?"

"I don't know. Maybe they'll ship us all out of here."

"You're crazy," Vernon said. "Think about those gilded bastards at the club last night. They *chose* to go there to fuck runts. What the hell is wrong with them?!"

"Runts like me!" Xaniel declared. "And I don't think anything *wrong* happened inside that Lovers' Closet, either."

"So, what?" Vernon said. "Now you're in a good mood again? Are their scraps all it takes for you to forget about everything?"

Xaniel sighed. "Cut me some slack, dude. Our friend Dayve is fucking dead. If he really killed someone famous, then life as we know it will never be the same.

That scares me."

"And you and I are right in the middle of it, too."

"There's no going back."

"Damn," Vernon said.

"So please," Xaniel added, "don't go radio-silent on me again. You're the only person I can really trust."

Vernon nodded, even as he felt himself being pulled further and further away by Ash's irresistible tide.

17. THAT FRAGILE TRUCE

Ash got home shortly after ten pm. She put the little treats she'd purchased from Eduardo into a hidden cubbyhole for another time. Tonight there would be no highs, no concubines, not even a replay with Vernon.

She had too much work to do, and needed time to think. Mercifully, Vernon hadn't made a scene when she let it be known that he was to be dropped off at home directly after leaving the police station. Ash hoped the gravity of the situation as laid out in Chief Paraquez's office, as well as seeing the department's complex inner workings, served as a reminder to Vernon that he was a passenger in all this and far out of his depth.

Back at the Towers, he'd simply gotten off the ATV and seemed about to wander off without a word, when she called his name. He turned back, casually brushing those precious bangs away from his eyes, and waited.

"Don't go taking any candy from strangers," she'd said. "I'm not through with you yet."

That brought out a little smile. He took a step toward her—for a kiss, or a hug?—but she just threw a soft punch at his arm, then revved the ATV away.

Ash didn't want to be seen giving pecks to a runt out on the street. Society's nuanced class distinctions had come about for a reason—their beautifully flourishing world of hemp and steel was the purpose and the proof— and maybe station-mixing was only tolerated as a stopgap between the species' chaotic past and its scheduled harmonious future.

Even a worker with municipal voting rights like Ash suspected that this seedy imbalance would at some point have to be phased out. The flawed and the inessential would be judged without pity before the gates of the future were officially opened. And those like her, who served as scaffolding during the transition, might also find themselves demoted once the new facade was complete.

Which explained why Ash was becoming increasingly obsessed with solving this new case, and even *hoping* a bigger conspiracy was involved. Because whoever cracked it wide open might earn themselves enough glory to reserve a space on the inside. Where surely there was more to life than punching derelicts, shopping for necklaces, and chasing sexual thrills through the forest of one's mind.

Ash stepped into the kitchen. It was nearly spotless for lack of use. She had neither the time nor the inclination to cook. Like construction and conception, food preparation was one of the many human tasks that had been outsourced, automated, and now done in bulk. Some bots down in the building's central kitchen—wearing frilly floral aprons, she hoped, but more likely just a collection of featureless machines—were busy stirring up the day's slop. All she had to do was tap a few sensor-buttons on the wall...

But she wasn't hungry. Too many important ideas

were floating around her mind to risk sinking into a food coma. Because from there she'd probably turn on the TV, and then, after seeing those beautiful people enjoying some form of leisure or pleasure, head out into the night herself.

She carried a tall cup of ice water to her standing workstation. The screen was big—forty-five inches from corner to corner—but didn't compare to what those gamers had.

She began her query: who really was Mallory Quentin? Now churning through data like a crab's mandibles in sand—her eyes and brain racing in a hundred different directions. A noted policy paper here. A career milestone there. Awards. Honors. Positions of power and responsibility. Everything above-board and without the scent of scandal. And then her horrific final moments at the Elixir Hotel...

As was always the case, speculation ran wild when someone prominent died unexpectedly. Which was why Ash held on to the notion of a micro-conspiracy—that this killing had to be motivated by more than just a broken heart or a jealous colleague.

But in truth, she knew virtually nothing about Mallory Quentin's private dealings. The woman had been a star player in the high-stakes game of reshaping the Earth. Was the murderer's true motivation part of some grand plot, like the anti-tech movement or marginalized men taking revenge?

Such groups had already tried that a few times, early on before Ash was a cop. Hacks into the system's mainframe trying to... what? Disable the bots altogether? Or reduce their efficiency, as if to impose a form of designed obsolescence in the era of perpetual motion?

Militias later attempted armed incursions when these surges of digital infiltration failed. But they were put down easily, and leaders were faced with the choice of whether to boldly publicize that the resistance had been quashed, or just sweep it all under the rug while the hi-tech juggernaut rolled along.

Even now, some of these granular details were accessible to Ash only because of her social rank and law enforcement credentials. The sliding scale of men in society—from second-class citizens with jobs on down to helpless wards of the state—meant that most were ignorant about the darker aspects of modern history. Women and girls, meanwhile, were taught and trained according to their aptitude and function as part of the sacred building mission.

Still, Ash couldn't shake her suspicion that the runts weren't all as clueless or stupid as the mainstream consensus held. Or was she only hoping so because this investigation affected her own future, and she was relying on cute little Vernon to help her solve it?

She decided to look into the connections between Naomi Blanchard and Mallory Quentin. They had both come out of Yale University's political science PhD program, whose rigorous curriculum was tailored toward real-world social justice applications. In 2026, each was tapped to join the Essential Planners, that two-hundred-strong managerial body of exceptional females recruited from across the professional spectrum.

For half an hour Ash researched the history of this remarkable group. First, there were the international symposiums where entire continents agreed to cede portions of their sovereignty in the service of a greater good—that promise of equitable prosperity and a lasting peace for all. In the ensuing years, many former EPs went on to head the specialized groups that formed to navigate the turbulent seas of change.

And here Ash felt the thread in her fingers give a little

tug. Because among their other duties and memberships, both Mallory Quentin and Naomi Blanchard had at one time been part of the trusted group that conducted diplomatic relations with the international drug cartels. Maintaining that fragile truce which had held firm for many years, and enabled each side to get what it wanted.

For the cartels it was customers, profit, securing their very existence in a time of decriminalized narcotics. For the world government, it was steady progress without a flood of too-powerful drugs that could rewire or subvert humanity, one smuggled kilo at a time.

Had something happened to destabilize this informal accord? The occasional bad batch or rogue tasty chef was one thing, but now a dangerous new pill was out on the streets—and one of the original Essential Planners was dead because of it.

Ash suddenly got chills. What would she find if she ran a name search on the nearly one thousand women who had served as EPs over the past two decades? Had any of *them* died recently? Or perhaps *other* accomplished women in positions of influence and power? How deep could it all possibly go—or was she allowing her ambitions to inflate what was really just one cleverly executed crime of passion?

She had to trust her abs that there was more going on here. Because it had been a fluke that she was at both crime scenes, something that the killer behind the killer could never have anticipated. Otherwise Dayve's death would have been the perfect cover. Just an everyday crime gone wrong. Another despicable runt doing what they do. Causing trouble. Crashing and burning. Testing society's patience once more.

Ash pictured Vernon's sleeping face in her mind...

She forced herself to step away from the workstation. She had wandered too far down the rabbit hole, and now logical thoughts were being overpowered by the fumes of speculation.

But as she prepared for bed, Ash held tight to one certainty: If her suspicions turned out to be correct, then her little life of local stardom and reckless nights was about to change. Whether she was vaulted into the worldwide spotlight as a hero, or left bleeding out as part of her own carefully staged death, she simply could not predict, or perhaps even control.

18. INTUITION

Ash felt herself yanked out of sleep by noises both in her room and somewhere off in the distance. Instinctively she threw out her arm and snatched her phone off the nightstand.

She cursed. It was Detective Gillard.

"What do you want?" she muttered.

"Knock, knock," the man said.

Ash heard several thumps on the front door of her apartment.

"Is that you outside my place?" Already she was rolling off the bed and onto her feet. "Who let you in the building?"

"It is I, the one and only! But I come bearing gifts. And big news."

"Yeah? I hope it's something shiny."

Ash didn't bother checking herself in the mirror or pulling her hair back. Gillard had seen her look much worse after doing battle with a rabid female suspect in a muddy field once.

She opened the apartment door. A coffee cup was thrust forward. A pastry bag shaken under her nose. She tucked her phone into the waistband of her panties, then took the coffee.

"Black," Gillard said. "Because *I know* how you like it."

Ash saw him give her body a once-over. Endless legs, cute little navel, breasts spilling out of a fuchsia bra. A prize he would never get.

"Speak or drool, Ted. What's your news?"

The man smiled. He said, "They found another body."

"What do you mean, *another?*"

"A second guest speaker from the Cheri Chat. Turned up dead this morning."

Ash spun on her heel and marched back into the apartment. She waved for Detective Gillard to follow her inside, then went into the bathroom.

"Talk to me," she called out as she began freshening herself up.

Gillard stood outside in the hallway and refrained from ogling her. "Donna Pearcey," he began. "Age fifty. Hosted two workshops on Saturday, then gave a speech yesterday. Found floating in a swimming pool, dead as a doornail."

"At the hotel?"

"Nope. If only it were that simple, Miss Westgard. Last night after the convention ended, she went out to stay with friends in Clay County. Everyone turned in around midnight, and then today, when the owner of the home carried her tea out onto the pool deck... That's when she found Ms. Pearcey. As for the fate of her mug, that remains unknown at this time."

Ash walked past him into the bedroom and put on fresh clothes. She said, "How do we know it wasn't just an accident?"

Again Gillard stood respectfully outside the door. He said, "Because the owners, the Yandells, have a top-of-the-line life-bot that's supposed to be on duty at all times. They discovered *it* powered down in a shed elsewhere on the property."

Ash was almost ready now. She adjusted her combat bra and spritzed her neck and chest with mango scent, then said, "So even when our victim jumped in the water, the bot didn't sense it and react?"

"They're running a scan on its activity log as we speak. We'll know soon enough. Whenever *we* get on the road, that is. Tick tock..."

"Yeah, yeah," Ash said while lacing up her boots.

It was a nearly forty-five-minute drive out to the Yandell residence. They rode in Detective Gillard's car because there was no way he could manage on the back of Ash's ATV with his bum prosthetic leg. She took the opportunity while playing passenger to pluck her eyebrows in the visor mirror.

"So, Gill," she said. "Any idea what you'll do with yourself when you retire?"

He gave a little laugh.

"Did you know, Ashley, that not everyone in the department is as eager to see me go as you are? I may not be able to run anymore, but when I use my mind... I *always* get my woman."

"You've been known to crack a few cases, I'll give you that. But you can't top female intuition. And with those new bot models joining the force... the upgraded SpideySense software... emotion filter upgrades... I just don't see how you'll be able to keep up."

Gillard glanced at her. She was filing her nails. He shook his head and declared, "Everything you say might be true, but they still haven't outsourced the job of being your babysitter."

"You little shit," Ash said. She jabbed the file into his thigh.

"Are you through? Because we're almost there. Time for you to pretend to be a detective again."

As the police cruiser eased into a long driveway, Ashley Westgard gritted her teeth and said, "I'll solve this murder—*these* murders, before you. Remember, I'm already one up."

"Pure luck," Gillard said. "And there's not a chance in hell your convenience store killer pulled *this* one off. Unless, of course, he reanimated at the morgue."

"Two dead Cheri Chatters," Ash said thoughtfully. "Two different killers. Gill, I really do think we might have a conspiracy on our hands!"

"Even *my* intuition told me that. Woman! Now let's get to work."

19. RULES OF THE HOUSE

The body was laid out under a sheet several yards from the water's edge. The pool surface wavered gently in the light morning breeze, and a green bird landed on one of the white beams that ran across the top of the screened-in deck.

Detective Ashley Westgard was alone. She paced down each side of the pool looking for any possible clues. But she knew very well that if this was indeed murder, the perpetrators would not have been so careless as to leave obvious tracks.

There were so many things she needed to know. But every question opened up on a network of trails, and pursuing the wrong ones would waste valuable time. Already the mastermind behind the first killing was clear by thirty-six hours. She could not afford to get lost in the wilderness.

Ash squatted down next to the body and pulled back the sheet. Donna Pearcey was wearing a one-piece navy swimsuit. *Okay, so she isn't naked. Or in street clothes.* No cuts or other surface wounds were visible. The medical examiner would have to determine if Pearcey had been hit on the head.

Ash went with the working theory that such elaborate planning and strategy meant that the drugged killer had personally drowned the victim. Perhaps he even did it in a bathtub inside the house, and then swapped out her clothes afterward. Or had she actually gone out for a swim? Such detailed questions were just more mental trails to get lost in—all that mattered was that Donna Pearcey was dead.

How, how, how? So many of Ash's questions started with that word. The logistics and the timetable behind the evil. She would only dare to wonder *why* much later.

She heard the sliding door open and looked up to see Detective Gillard wave her inside. Carefully she laid the sheet back in place, then entered the house. Earlier she had made a beeline from the front door straight to the pool deck, but now Ash fully took in its character.

Money. Old money. Class. Taste in sculpture and paintings. Antique furniture in the Southern style. A shelf loaded with old books by great historical thinkers, both male and female. A wet bar supplied with only classic liqueurs. The place was a time capsule.

Ted Gillard was now escorting an elderly woman into the room, and allowing her to lean against him for support. Ash hoped for everyone's sake that his leg didn't give out.

The woman extended her hand to Ash, saying in a shaky voice, "Please forgive my nerves. As you must surely understand, we've all had a terrible shock."

"But of course, ma'am," Ash said. Unconsciously she zipped her hoodie fully closed. "I'm very sorry about what happened. Now, I know you've already spoken to the other officers, but would you mind answering just a few of my questions?"

"Anything I can do to help find out what happened to Donna. But please, I must sit down."

Ash and Gillard helped the woman into a creamy gold chair with velvety texture.

"What is your name, ma'am?" Ash asked. "And how did you know Ms. Pearcey?"

The old woman shook her head sadly. "Jane Yandell. Retired professor emeritus from Yale University. That's where I met Donna all those years ago. She and many of the others who went on to lead during the great transformation."

Ash sat in a wicker chair beside Jane. She said, "My name is Ashley Westgard. I'm a detective with the JPC. I hate to add to your troubles, but we have reason to believe that foul play may have been involved in Donna's death."

"Yes, the others just told me. I of course read in the papers about poor Mallory Quentin, but somehow I didn't make the connection until just now. It's all been so distressing."

"Ms. Yandell, did you hear or see anything suspicious during the night or early this morning?"

"Not at all. Everything was as normal as ever. I have guests here from time to time. Nothing out of the ordinary happened."

"I see," Ash said. "And how long in advance was Donna's visit planned?"

"Well, in case you aren't aware, this Cheri Chat convention has grown into something quite prestigious. Donna signed on as a speaker months ago. And we finalized plans for her visit here at least two weeks back."

"Is there anyone else here in the house, ma'am?"

"Yes," Jane said, "two others. First, my husband Horace. He's five years my senior and much worse for wear at the moment. Then there is my maid and attendant

Laura, who has been with me for nearly fifteen years. It is unfathomable to me that she would be capable of murder." The old woman shuddered.

Ash took one of the lady's hands into her own and said, "Had Laura and Donna met before?"

"But certainly! Donna has stayed here several times."

"Is there any possibility of... a liaison between them? One that perhaps went sour overnight?"

"Heavens no," Mrs. Yandell said, snatching away her hand. "Laura knows very well the rules of the house. Despite my reputation as a *progressive* thinker, in some ways I am still very much an old-fashioned woman. We *must* maintain certain levels of distinction, otherwise one transgression leads to another. After that, it's only a matter of time before everything dissolves into a mess down on the floor."

"But Donna," Ash continued, "she was a powerful woman. Perhaps she held sway over Laura, and you just didn't see it?"

"Never! Detective, I believe you're barking up the wrong skirt—and wasting valuable time—if indeed my poor Donna is the second victim."

Ash relented. She said, "I just had to be certain. Please forgive me for asking these difficult questions."

Just then Detective Gillard, who had slipped out of the room to give the women privacy, returned holding a sheet of paper.

"Ash?" he said. "I think we should go have a look at the life-bot."

She thanked Jane for her time and then followed Ted out onto the property. The shed sat a hundred feet away from the pool deck under a cluster of oak and dogwood trees. It was spacious enough to house a large self-driving lawnmower, two work benches, and a variety of tools, boxes, and pool supplies.

And over in the far corner sat the life-bot with its arms clasped around tucked knees, looking like a mannequin performing a cannonball.

Gillard rustled his paper. "Look at this," he said. "The unit's internal activity log notes that the pool was being drained for crack sealing. The instructions say the bot's services wouldn't be required for several days."

Ash glanced at the printout, then said, "You've confirmed with the maid that no such maintenance orders were placed?"

"You got it."

"Look, any bot can get glitchy or tie itself into logical knots. Happens all the time. Are we *completely* sure this wasn't just a terrible coincidence?"

"Ashley, you know as well as I do that Donna Pearcey was not the victim of bad luck, or even a freak accident."

Ash stepped back out into the yard. With hands on hips she surveyed the majestic Yandell property.

"Gill, I'm glad you're on board with my original theory. But maybe you don't yet fully grasp the implications of what's going on here. Someone has just killed two of the most prominent female thinkers of our time. What if this is just the beginning of who-knows-how-many assassinations?"

Detective Gillard said, "Why would anyone want to do that?"

"You mean, what would be the motive? Good luck poking around that haystack! Anyway, the next thing I need to do is learn more about the connection between Mallory Quentin and Donna Pearcey. And I know just the person to ask."

20. HER ULTIMATE FEAR

Naomi Blanchard was a nervous wreck. Two friends and colleagues going back decades were suddenly dead. *Had been killed!* Was she next?

The odds seemed against it. She was one visitor among hundreds when she'd gone to watch Mallory Quentin's presentation at the Cheri Chat. The convention roster itself was stacked with the leading female names in science, politics, and the arts. The crowds were a sea of civil servants and students who all worked toward their common goal. Surely no one was interested in targeting her, a member of the old guard who had left public life to pursue boutique projects?

Besides, Naomi thought, certainly *someone* had died during one of the previous Cheri Chat weekends? Perhaps a little late-night kink taken too far, or a drunken reveler falling off a balcony? Those types of accidents happened all the time at hotels. But murder? It was all so shocking!

Naomi pulled on her quilted floral cotton jacket, standing before the hallway mirror as she slowly fastened the wooden toggles. She still had to live life despite her fears—and right now her two precious dogs needed their exercise.

She opened a nearby drawer, clicking her tongue as she held up the leashes and called, "Tinsley! Marlow! Come now!"

There was the thump of feet upon the replica Turkish rug in the dining room, and then nails clicking against the main foyer's gray stone floor. Naomi rubbed the floppy ears of these statuesque standard poodles with affection, then secured the clasp of a leash onto each of their collars.

She stepped out into the comfortable midday air. Her house was one of hundreds that dotted the winding streets of this suburban neighborhood built back in the 1970s. She liked the balance of personal space and sense of community here. Quaint game nights. Lively cocktail socials. And even the occasional children's game played out in someone's front yard.

But Naomi particularly enjoyed the little forest that developers hadn't been able to get at when creating this grid of two-story homes and cul-de-sacs. It was now a pleasant network of crisscrossing trails, complete with chirping birds and squirrels that skittered from tree to tree in playful chase.

Tinsley and Marlow lurched forward as Naomi turned into one of the entry points. Once inside the woods, she let them off their leashes and watched as they scampered in pursuit of some critter that was rustling under dead leaves within a cluster of bushes.

She felt *nice* here. Far away from the constricting walls of the office, where she was always looking over her shoulder and waiting for someone to call her out for only giving *the impression* of working. Or perhaps being taken to task for her little acts of sabotage. Maybe the system had quietly been tallying up her petty crimes, and would now send her back to France to live among her ancestral cousins as punishment. Oh well, she might enjoy passing the rest of her days quietly tending to grape vines in those rustic fields, knowing that she had already changed the world...

Because truth be told, Naomi Blanchard found herself vaguely anxious even when sitting inside her own lovely home. Despite all the aesthetic art and expensive furniture and tasteful interior design, there was an emptiness within the fullness.

She had gotten everything she ever wanted in life and in her career, but it was here, while walking these forest paths, that Naomi felt most at peace. This preserve whose carpeting of pine needles was created by nature, rather than foreign fingers in the cruel sweatshops of last century, or the blindingly fast robots inside today's rug factories. Here her seat was an uneven stone which waited patiently for wanderers in need of a brief rest, instead of the ergonomic office chair that was meticulously designed to extract the most possible work from her.

These woods were a place where small animals and the creek that meandered through it were all the entertainment one needed. So different from the cacophonous programs on television, which were a carefully crafted mix of political talking points, sexual arousal, and soap-opera melodrama.

Sometimes Naomi wanted to stay here surrounded by the spread arms of these lovely trees, and never return to the outside world. Because her greatest fear, after straining for so long beneath the Sword of Damocles, was that nothing would happen if it fell. Meaning that a threshold had been crossed, and there was no need for high priestesses or even kings anymore. Everything was set to cruise control—and surely the system would prefer that nervous feet refrained from tapping on the brakes unnecessarily.

She called out to the dogs, then turned onto the portion of the path that would take her to the creek. Tinsley and Marlow caught up and now trotted along beside her. She scratched them on the back of their necks as they glanced from side to side in search of the next squirrel to chase.

For a moment, Naomi envisioned that the ghosts of Mallory Quentin and Donna Pearcey were also here walking with her. The Turning Point Sisters. That's what they had been called when as a trio they'd penned the groundbreaking feasibility study, "Finding a Way Forward, Offering a Way Out: Managing the Implications of Innovation and Decriminalization."

It was back in the fall of 'twenty-five, when they were all doctoral students at Yale. While their spirits were buoyed by the cresting wave of female empowerment, their minds danced with macro visions of how to interweave hard infrastructure with humanity's ethereal dreams—and find the delicate balance between these two forces.

Their stunning document, cooked up over several months between tipsy brunches and short-term boyfriends —back when dating was still done in the *old* way—it had launched them overnight onto the global stage as serious philosophers who would help guide the world forward. They were soon nominated to serve as Essential Planners, and the rest was history—as chronicled in textbooks and visible to the eye across ten thousand cities.

Naomi, Mallory, and Donna eventually went on to have different careers within the same larger sphere, yet they always stayed in touch and held semi-annual reunions. But not this year, and never again. The lovely dinner they intended to share this very night had been canceled by an evil force.

She reached the little stream and took the path that ran along its bank. The dogs danced at the water's edge, occasionally dipping their snouts in to drink or bite at something beneath the surface.

She felt a whoosh of air go past her right side. There was a tug on her sleeve. The leaves in front of her kicked up and the dogs darted forward.

Naomi touched her upper right arm. The fabric was torn. Her fingers came up wet and red. Now there was a hard pressure against her back. She looked down—a triangular piece of metal had ripped through the front of her jacket. One of the toggles was splintered.

She fell to her knees, suddenly feeling weak and worried that she might not be able to get the expanding stain out of her nice jacket.

The dogs were with her as she slumped over onto her side. She reached out to grab them, or maybe feel the pine needles, wondering why she was so sleepy in this forest which she cherished so much.

21. UNHEALTHY DESIRES

"Damn."

Ash tossed her phone onto the floor mat.

"No dice?" Gillard pulled the police cruiser into a turning lane.

"They say she's taking a personal day. But that's alright. We got other work to do."

"Us, or the computers?"

Ash looked out the window. She said, "We have to trace this second killer coming *and* going. How and when did he make his way up to the house? Was he programmed to self-destruct too?"

"Assuming your idea about the *terminator tasties* is even right."

"That's cute, Ted. But yes, it's what I'm going off. Then, after we get a bead on him, the system needs to track him *back further* to the moment when he got his pill."

"Or *she*," Gillard added. "Murder is an equal-opportunity inclination, my friend."

"Yeah, maybe. But don't bet your cane on it."

"My walking stick... or my *night* stick?"

Ash shook her head doubtfully. "Gill, the only part of your body we can rely on to never stop working is your mouth."

"God, I'd hate to end up on your shit list..."

By the time Detective Gillard dropped Ash back at her apartment building, she was ready to run with another idea. She logged into the department's database and started learning about the tasty trader known as Clarkus.

Clarence Kenneth Rialto. Age twenty-three. Mixed-race with a little bit of everything—including a few battle scars on his face. Originally from the Allapattah area of Miami. Member of the Jacksonville nano-pusher network for nearly three years. He had kept a fairly clean record except for a few hit-and-runs and physical altercations which the city declined to prosecute. It was easier for law enforcement to keep tabs on a known roster of semi-volatile types, rather than create openings for potentially sociopathic newcomers to fill.

Ash munched on the pastry that Gill had brought over earlier while she dug into the file. One side of her brain was thinking about how many reps she'd have to do in kickboxing class to keep her ass and thighs from ballooning, while the other plotted out the ways she might catch young Clarkus in the act.

He mainly kept to a six-block radius within the larger area where much of the city's worst offenders congealed. Poorly lit underpasses, forgotten walkways, and crumbling buildings were their playground.

Clarkus and his ilk sold escape to all takers. A vault up for the defeated. Something *unique* for those who could afford to purchase anything their eyes desired. And blissful forgetfulness for the gilded who lived like idle kings, but still felt that something was missing from their lives.

But now there was someone else, someone *different* poking around. Stirring up the waters. And that simply didn't happen by chance. Traders were more territorial than even the most possessive butch lesbian Ash had ever squared off against—because as hypnotic as young pussy was, it was still plentiful and cheap. Whereas turf, product, and respect... That was what these salesmen who lived in the shadows fought to protect at all cost.

Ash put in a system request to trace Clarkus's movements going back to Saturday morning. The high-speed scan would create a zigzagging map of his footsteps during this window of time.

If all went smoothly, within two hours she might have a visual on the mysterious out-of-towner who had supplied Dayve—and possibly one other person—with his tasty. She could only hope that the man's face wasn't obscured or altered, and that he was in the international ID system. Otherwise they were chasing a killer with no name and no motive.

The next response in that case would be to start turning the screws into Clarkus himself—and after that, leaning on the wider circle of traders. But that would all take time. Meanwhile the killer's trail would be getting colder and colder.

The department would surely resist doing it like that anyway. City bureaucracy was always hesitant about disrupting the symbiotic relationship it had with certain shady characters. Because apparently, Ash now realized, the criminal element was in fact *an integral part* of that steam valve which aided the larger mission toward progress.

But with two high-profile murders on its hands, the Jacksonville Police Corps might have no choice but to cast disinfecting sunlight onto some of the no-go zones, however temporarily. Otherwise they could all be in for a real comeuppance if, say, some outside regulator looking to make her bones started poking around the city's affairs.

Ash also wondered how long it would take for the FBI to get involved. No doubt the League of Female Leaders would apply pressure for any and all resources to be dedicated to apprehending whoever had killed two of their honorary members.

Suddenly she began to feel a bit ill. The accolades she envisioned receiving for helping to solve a single murder were slipping away in the wake of it all turning into a much bigger case. One that was maybe too complex for a detective who still used her fists as much as her brain—and who shamelessly relied on her partner to do much of the leg work, while she was hanging out at the fitness center doing leg workouts.

Her personal phone pinged. A message from Vernon. He wanted to see her again. She kind of did too—if only to take her mind off this work stress, which was crashing down on her plans like a ton of bricks.

But still... What was up with all these men in her life?! How could it even be *possible* now? This was a woman's world, and no one doubted the fact. Ash herself was in her prime at age twenty-seven: old enough to sweep an innocent chick under her arm, but also still able to play princess for an older executive who wanted to treat her to a good time.

Was that really what she had felt when sitting across the desk from Naomi Blanchard? Was their momentary connection nothing more than common flirting? Or, had they truly stumbled onto some yearning that was deeper than what splashes of wine and nights in satin sheets could satisfy?

Detective Ashley Westgard was at a loss. She never imagined she would feel uncertain about so many things, especially at this point in her life. She simply took for

granted that every achievement and life experience moved her along a linear path toward confidence, understanding, and ultimately power. It was inevitable, or so she had thought until now.

She left her desk and went to the corner of the living room where she kept her workout supplies. She flipped ahead in the "Beach Babes on the Beat" wall calendar to her month. There she was. Bright blue bikini. Glistening in oil. Hair tumbling down freely. A pistol in her right hand. Cuffs in the other. Looking so knowingly at the camera—and deep into everyone's soul.

Was it all a lie? The people who personally admired her, and those who just fantasized about the alluring woman in this perfect picture... Would they not even care what internal struggles this sex object was going through? Would they rip out the page in disgust at her hypocrisy or put-upon attitude? Or would they affect a sympathetic tone, then try to lead her away to their bedroom for comfort?

She let the pages of the calendar fall in dismay. Nothing was clear. Nothing was pure. Everyone had an angle. No one simply *was*. Because with all basic human needs provided for by a world that was running on autopilot, people's *wants* and *interests* had metastasized into compulsions and unhealthy desires.

Ash now saw that she, like so many others, had been using the Seven Deadly Sins as personal lifestyle accessories. They had all stripped down naked and eased into a boiling cauldron of iniquity, laughing and splashing each other as they melted inside this toxic bitches brew. And if it proved rarely fatal, that was only because technology, plentiful food, and top-level medical care made for such a resilient safety net.

Thus it was that twenty years after humanity's crowning achievement, its leaders and beneficiaries had become more degenerate than Rome. But still, the mechanized support staff remained on call to scrub the floors clean, replace the dented fenders, and even set out an aspirin in the morning without passing judgment.

Perhaps this spiritual cancer was undetectable by the literal-minded network of computers that ran the world. Meanwhile, the corrupted gray cells were not so little anymore. They were growing to unsustainable proportions behind every injected lip that smiled for selfies, under piles of stomach fat glued to sofa cushions, and inside poisoned hearts craving for new depths of sin.

Ash exhaled heavily. She stood there looking out the balcony window at nothing.

Some moments later she heard a beep back in her little office. It would be a relief and a blessing if the results of the Clarkus query were complete. She needed something productive to focus on, instead of stewing in dark thoughts.

But she froze when she saw the new message. It had nothing to do with her information request at all.

Naomi Blanchard, perhaps the only other woman who sensed the horrors lurking within their picturesque future world, was dead.

A crossbow's arrow had pierced her through.

Ashley Westgard, the pin-up calendar girl, fell to her knees and began to cry for the first time in years.

22. INEXHAUSTIBLE HATE

Ash could feel her fury and rage turning white hot. All the grief that made her want to squeeze her eyes and weld them shut forever was being redirected into the molten core of her soul.

It was in this moment that the wildly divergent elements that made up Ashley Westgard were being forged into something mightier than she had ever been before. Focus, purpose, and an inexhaustible supply of primal hatred were ready to be unleashed with the lethal precision of a laser beam in the name of justice.

She stepped out of the shower spa and activated the air jets. Nude, she stood before the mirror and worked aloe gel into her skin. She leaned in close and applied silver streaks of eyeliner. And with the immaculate care of a funeral director, she wove her blond locks into two tight Dutch braids.

She went to her wardrobe closet, sliding the hangers slowly from right to left. Finally she lifted one off the rod, letting it spin on two fingers while she considered her options. New with tags, this was the last of the six dark teal sparkling combat bras she had purchased a month ago.

Carefully she snipped away the labels, then eased the bra over her head and scooped her breasts inside. Next she inserted ribbed foam pads into the thighs of a pair of smoky-gray knee-length stretch pants, before stepping into them and yanking firmly on the D-rings of the canvas belt.

She selected a pair of leather boots in deep charcoal. The steel toes protruded like a lurking menace, and the groove-edged rubber soles were a sickly shade of yellow-brown. There was no fur lining inside. These boots had only one purpose: to seek and destroy.

Ash walked into the kitchen serenely, with back arched and arms hanging limp at her sides. She slid a bottle of vodka out of the freezer and filled a tumbler glass nearly to the lip. She gulped it down and whipped her head from side to side. It was go time.

Pistol. Phone. Bracelet. Badge. Gum. Mace. Lip gloss. Silver leather jacket. A glaze of determination within dead eyes.

Next, marching out to her ATV in the garage. Not even acknowledging the neighbors who smiled as they passed. Feeling her every deliberate action fed by a steady IV drip of concentrated, righteous anger.

Now downloading all of the Clarkus data from her computer into the ATV's system. Dropping a pin on his location and requesting updates on his movements from the police department's mainframe. Because they had a date with destiny—he just didn't know it yet.

Night was falling on the City of Jacksonville. A phantom on a smoke-colored ATV whizzed through the immaculate streets, the braids of her helmetless head whipping in the wind and dancing against her shoulders. Her eyes—obsessed and hidden behind black goggles—

bore down on the incorrigible danger zone where a killer had set up shop.

The beacon on her dash screen showed that Clarkus remained inside his normal field of play. With several blocks to go, she instructed the computer to provide as much detailed information about his location as was available.

The results: indoors, second floor, in the living room of a two-bedroom apartment. Sitting on his ass watching television.

"Of course he is," she said aloud to herself.

She parked in an alley around the corner from his building. Then she spent several minutes crouching low and observing the street scene before stepping out onto the sidewalk.

Within seconds she saw some guy in a plaid shirt that came down to his knees sidle up next to her. He must have watched her drive into the alley and then hung around until she finally emerged. Now he rubbed his hands together.

"Hey lady," he said. "I can be your new naughty secret, if you want."

Ash stopped walking. She slit her eyes and said, "Fuck —you. And fuck—off."

The man stepped back, raising his hands defensively. "Or maybe you just need something to take off the edge?"

"Stick around and I'm gonna *take off* your goddamn head."

"Naw, you wouldn't do that..."

"And bring it home with me as a souvenir. For my collection."

"You're crazy, girl. Sick in *your* head..." He swatted his hand at nothing and wandered off into the darkness.

As Ash turned her attention back to the mission, she was secretly thankful for this little encounter. It had alerted her senses and provided a quick adrenaline boost before the unknowns of battle.

She slipped into Clarkus's building easily. The metal frame of the cracked-glass front door was so warped that it could barely even be pulled shut. Silently she moved up a staircase that had chunks missing from the steps, gashes in the walls, and empty bottles scattered on the middle landing.

Quickly and quietly she moved down the second floor hallway. It was very dim, with only two functioning bulbs. Rips and stains ran down the length of the thin-shaved carpeting. She put an ear to the apartment door— TV on loud, a voice laughing.

She glanced at the screen on her bracelet. It said that there was only one person inside the unit. To kick, knock, or pop—that was the question. She inspected the door fixture. It was a standard brass lock, but that could be misleading. Even if traders didn't always keep product or money at home, they still valued their safety.

Ash decided to enter with a bang. She reached into the waist pack she'd taken from her ATV's storage box and removed a one-inch-diameter olive tube. She unscrewed the cap and wiped the greasy tip around the perimeter of the door. She tripled the coat across the top, then deftly ran a fine wire around the frame and diagonally from corner to corner.

She stepped away and ducked, covering her head as she pressed a red plastic button that was attached to the end of the wire. She heard a loud crack that sounded like a two-by-four hitting a table, and then the door slammed down from top to bottom.

Instantly she was up with pistol drawn. She leaped inside onto the fallen door and howled, "Clarkus! Police! Don't you move a fucking muscle!"

Ash saw through the haze that the man had flung

himself off the couch and was trying to swim across the floor back toward the bedrooms. She moved into the darkened apartment cautiously, weapon aimed squarely at his back.

"Now listen," she said. "It may not look like it right now, but I'm not here to come down on you. So if you tell me what I want to hear, then it means no jail and no body bag. Got it?"

Clarkus slowly rolled onto his back, hands up in self-defense. "I ain't wanna die, lady," he said. "I'll give up the stash, no problem."

"I don't want your garbage. Now get up, go lean that door against the frame. Then we're gonna talk. Okay, move nice and slow. There you go..."

Ash swiveled around as Clarkus got to his feet and hoisted up the door. He wedged it semi-closed, then stepped to the side with his hands open in front of his chest. Now she saw the inside of the door for the first time, and indeed there were extra security features not visible from the hall. Had she tried to kick it in, she would have received a hail of bullets or given Clarkus time to escape out a back window.

"Have a seat," Ash said. She motioned to the couch. "Hands on your knees, that's it. Now, Clarkus. Word is that you've been introducing a new guy to the neighborhood. From my understanding, that's not how it's normally done. I believe one of the other corner jockeys has to leave first, breathing or not, before that happens. So what gives?"

Clarkus pinched the fabric of his dark sweatpants. He said, "I can't speak to any of that. Outside arrangements were made. I'm just the tour guide."

"Who made these arrangements? And where is your friend from?"

Clarkus started to rub the top of his fuzzy head, then

grimaced as he put his hand back onto his leg. "Fuck me... Fuck *this*... And where you at? FBI, DEA? *UN?* Or just a cop?"

"What does that matter to you?" Ash said. "*I* got the drop, so *you* gotta talk."

"Why it matter? 'Cause it's all about how much you know. And how much a person *got* to know. Before maybe, well, you're worth more dead than alive."

"Like I said, I'm not here to take you out. I want the bigger fish."

"But what if I'm already dead?" Clarkus said. "Somebody else sees that this door came down, maybe they spread the word I got caught up. Lady, I need protection right now!"

Ash felt a cold rivulet of the unknown trickle down and sizzle against her roaring engine. Was this kid playing games, or revealing that the waters she'd stepped into were much deeper than she had expected?

"I just need a name," she said. "A number or a location. You gotta give me something before I can offer you any help. You understand, right?"

Clarkus shook his head, giving a sad smile as he said, "I'm a *trader*. Can't be giving no freebies away now, not when it's my neck on the line."

"Please, just tell me, how do you two meet? Who sets it up?"

"He always ready. Just waitin' on me to find the right customer."

"What does that even mean? Who's doing the buying?"

"Man, you know we sell to all types. Well, *he* only want to meet the losers... the runts. So I got to wait for one of them to call me."

Ash saw a vision of the heavens open up in her mind. A bulbous tower of silvery clouds parting to reveal the blazing sun in all its majesty.

"Clarkus, you beautiful son of a bitch," she said. "You may have earned yourself a deal after all."

"Oh yeah?" he said. "Truth?"

"Yes, sir. Because you just gave me an idea."

23. LIVE BAIT

"I still cannot believe you forced my hand like this, *Ashley*."

Chief of Detectives Gabriela Paraquez was adjusting the sides of her ballistic vest. The letters JPC were stenciled in white across the back.

"I just felt the walls closing in," Ash said.

"On us all? Or only yourself? Because there's a difference between taking initiative and utter recklessness."

Ash now chose her words carefully. Much more so than her actions of two hours ago, which had jump-started the tactical response team into rapid action.

"Chief, sometimes I think our gut instinct is one of the only things these bots will never figure out. They'll spend all day crunching numbers looking for the perfect odds before they act. Meanwhile the suspect could be running away under their noses."

"Are you shitting me?" Paraquez said. She pointed at the two robot cops standing at the entrance of this small, tucked-away base camp. "They're here to protect *all* our asses. Why you went off like a cowgirl without telling anybody, or at least bringing one of them along as backup... You could've gotten yourself killed!"

Ash decided not to say anything more. She had gotten her way. It was only fair to get chewed out for what she had done—and was about to set in motion.

"And another thing," Paraquez said, giving Ash a sideways glance. "You didn't even bother to let Gill know this was going down, did you?"

Ash smirked. "We couldn't have that gimpy old timer getting in the way, right?"

"Detective Westgard. That man is a police—"

"What he is, is *less* than a man."

"You're really having a time tonight, aren't you? Just be ready to answer the bell. I've got some work to do, excuse me."

After Paraquez moved away, Ash turned her attention to a zip pack that was resting on a cinder block wall. Inside were the tactical supplies that she didn't normally carry. Anti-glare goggles, ballistic vest, radio with dedicated channels—and greasepaint. She wiped two black streaks beneath each eye. *Hell yeah.*

She walked into the command center after she was loaded up. Over a dozen uniformed women, bots, and men were milling around the garage of this abandoned townhouse. Computers on folding tables gave views of nearby streets and structures.

"Okay!" a seated tech called out. "We've got movement. Boss?"

Chief Paraquez and another high-ranking female officer leaned in and scanned the screens. At the same moment Paraquez tapped her ear, glancing down and nodding her head.

"Roger that," she said quietly, then turned to address the room. "Heads up, people! Our scouts are confirming visual. Move out... it's showtime!"

The seedy streets were a rare kind of quiet that maybe only happened once a week. Monday after midnight and no one was out carousing. Everyone had expended all their energy, and money, between Thursday evening and the wee hours of Sunday night. Even the most dedicated partiers were catching up on their rest now.

Only the animals that never knew what day it was, and the far-gone derelicts who had long since given up such conventions, were out roaming now.

Vernon had left his dorm room on foot fifteen minutes prior. Before that, he had been comfortably entrenched in his gaming chair, with a cold beverage at his side and expecting to play all through the night.

Then a call had come in. Lighting up a corner of his giant TV screen. Lighting up his soul.

From where he stood now, he could just see the top of one of the Towers between several nearby trees and apartment buildings. He was getting nervous. Would *she* show up as promised? Could he really go through with the things she had demanded of him?

He hadn't told Xaniel about this. Despite the promise he made to keep him in the loop, Vernon couldn't in good conscience put his friend's life in danger. Not when in his heart, he knew he was doing this as much for Ash as for Dayve.

He heard a clicking sound to his right. Out of the darkness a hand waved at him from behind a chain-link fence. He raced over.

"Are you Mister V?" a voice whispered.

"Yeah," Vernon said.

"You alone?"

"Uh-huh."

"Okay, keep quiet and follow me."

Vernon ran after the other man. They went down the side of a long three-story apartment building that was shrouded in darkness, then came to an uneven brick patio next to an overgrown yard.

"Wait here," the man said.

Vernon felt his heart begin to pound. A few distant street lights and the subtle glow of the night sky were all he could rely on to make sense of his surroundings. It was deadly quiet. He prayed that he hadn't walked into a trap. He didn't want to die alone behind some empty tenement house. In that moment the Towers seemed very precious to him—at least they still had life inside.

Another series of clicks came at him as the man returned.

"You got your payment?"

"Yeah, but—"

"Hand it over. Now."

Vernon had no choice. If he was truly a dead man, it made no difference whether he gave up the money now or had it yanked out of his pocket after being disposed of.

"Come on," the other man said. "He's just inside."

Vernon again followed, this time entering the rear of the building. One searing silvery bulb hung in the far left corner of a rectangular room. A second man stood in the shadows, a silhouette separated from the door by a thousand tiny floor tiles.

"Ah," this man said. "Here's our next customer."

The first trader hustled Vernon forward into the blinding light. He said, "All paid up, sir."

"Yes, of course. Now, Clarkus, where did you find this one?"

"They know me up in the Towers. Word gets around, I guess. Provide that endurance, that confidence, whatever they need."

"I see." The shadow turned to Vernon. "So tell me,

friend. What are you in the mood for?"

Vernon licked his lips. He said, "I like to, uh... float. Feel smooth."

"Understandable. Do you ever rocket?"

"Yeah, sometimes. But not out of nowhere, right? A good tasty ramps you up, it doesn't just launch you."

The man chuckled. "Okay, you know your stuff. But... what if I could offer you the night of your life? Would you take it?"

Vernon blinked in the glare. He felt the imposing presence of these two faceless men, knowing that he was completely alone and at their mercy. They could slit his throat in this forgotten laundry room and no one would find his body for weeks.

"Well?" the man in silhouette said.

Vernon saw Clarkus adjust his weight nervously. He looked at the man again and said, "What do you call it?"

"Funny. Everyone wants to know the name, rather than simply enjoy the privilege of being a tasty tester."

"Oh," Vernon said. "Okay. If it's new, and it's hot, I'll try it."

"Excellent decision."

The man extended his hand directly under the light, palm facing up. Vernon saw a large textured pill resting on top of a square of paper. He picked up the tasty and then looked more closely at what was underneath. It was the formal picture of a smiling woman in a business suit.

Suddenly the hand clasped shut and crumpled the photograph. The man lowered his arm and eased further back into the corner.

"Our business is finished," he said. "Clarkus, please escort our friend back to the street."

As Vernon stuffed the tasty into his pocket, he felt Clarkus push him forcefully out of the room into the blackness of the night. The instant his feet touched the outside pavement, all hell broke loose.

First an insane electronic squawking sound filled the air. He was disoriented and staggered out toward the brickwork, but then a figure that was running past slammed into him heavily.

He twisted and fell, landing on his back and now facing the building. The scene was a blur of crisscrossing lights. People and robots were sprinting in all directions. Throughout the chaos, the awful noise persisted.

And then he saw her. Arms pumping. Surging forward with war paint on her cheeks. Colors flashing off the lenses of her goggles. The ends of those beautiful braids peeking out from inside a black helmet. She pointed and shouted something at a bot, then whipped her head toward the scene at the back door.

There was a crush of bodies with one pinioned man in front. She launched forward and clawed at him like a mountain cat, until finally she was torn away by other officers and subdued in the weeds.

Vernon reached out a hand to touch her wrist. The cacophony had stopped. But his being was so focused on her that he remained nearly deaf.

She looked up at him, for a moment not recognizing his face or even seeing that anyone was there. But he continued to stare at her without fear.

Suddenly she pulled her goggles away and lunged into his arms.

"You did it," she said lovingly, looking down into his eyes and caressing his cheeks. "You helped save the day."

He let his head fall back. He gazed up at the night sky as she patted and rubbed his chest.

Vernon had avenged his friend Dayve's death. And his dream girl had been there to witness it all. Life could be so good sometimes...

24. SPILLING HIS GUTS

The man in the hot seat seemed unfazed by the violent sequence of events that had led him into this interrogation room. He wore a shimmering black suit, and his slender face was elegant—but Ash could clearly see that there were strong cheekbones underneath his youthful skin.

She was standing on the opposite side of the two-way mirror in the adjoining room. At her side was Chief of Detectives Paraquez, as well as several other high-ranking police officials she had never met before. They watched as Investigator Randall Ellis stalked his prey.

"That's a nice suit," Ellis remarked. "A bit fancier than what I'm used to seeing you traders wear."

The other man smiled. "I happen to be a traveling salesman. Proper attire is essential."

"Oh yeah? From where? And what are you offering that's so different from what's on the street now?"

"I think you already know that."

Investigator Ellis jabbed a finger close to the suspect's face. He said angrily, "Then there's no reason for you to act so smug. You're looking at murder... violating international nanotech accords... maybe even hate crimes. And that's just for starters."

"Violating? No, I would say 'transcending' is the more appropriate term."

"You know something? I do like this performance of yours. So serene and calm. But still, you got caught, son! You're gonna spend the rest of your life behind bars. It's over!"

The prisoner brought cuffed hands up to smooth his black hair. Parted down the center, it had been mussed during his arrest and now would not stay in place. A small piece of tissue clung to the scratch mark on his forehead that Detective Westgard had inflicted in the scuffle.

He said, "Do you really think this ends with me? No disrespect to your little city, but it's not exactly a New York or a Los Angeles." He gave a mischievous smile.

"Say what now?" Ellis said. "What exactly are you getting at?"

"Pardon, but I think I'm done talking for the moment. I'd like a lawyer and a deal. I talk? I walk. Do you understand?"

Ellis approached the mirror and swirled his finger in the air for those watching on the other side of the glass. Then he turned back, saying, "We can arrange something, sure. But just tell me why. Why did you kill those women? So respected and beloved, and now they're gone."

"You expect me to feel sympathy for *them?*" the suspect said. "After they spent their lives fostering imbalance? Never!"

"You and your goddamn riddles. But you know what pisses me off the most? The cowardly way you went about it all. Using others to do your dirty work for you. Disgusting!"

"Please, spare me. Let's not pretend that any of you actually cared about... my instruments."

"Who the fuck are you?!" Ellis exploded. "You won't give us your name. Face, fingerprints, and blood don't come up in any of our systems, some-fucking-how. And yet you descend upon *our* city with an agenda. A grudge!"

"Who I am is unimportant. What I represent should concern you, however. Because you all have been put on notice!"

"What the hell are you talking about?" Ellis was clenching his fists in frustration. "Please just spit it out, because I am truly interested."

The young man straightened his tie. He said, "The fact is, our uncles only ever understood the *business* side. Money and operations. They were never concerned about what the product was, so long as it kept selling. But conditions change. Products change. *Times* change. And so now, maybe the products will influence the conditions."

"Listen, you slick bastard, I've dealt with every type of lowlife out there. This act of yours doesn't impress me."

"How can I make you see? We are the new kings. Meaning that you aren't just on your heels, but lying flat on your back. We have the means, and we have that which our greedy and shortsighted fathers did not—the will."

"But how can a king such as yourself rule from prison?" Ellis said.

The suspect smiled. He said, "The whole world has become a giant open-air prison. We're trying to set everyone free."

"With drugs that cause innocent people to kill? You are truly one sick puppy!"

The prisoner raised his hands and shook them so that

his jacket sleeves eased away from the handcuffs. He checked the time on his watch, then said, "You know something? I don't believe I'll be needing that lawyer after all. But could I please trouble you for a last cup of coffee? I take it with cream."

"Last?" the investigator said. "As in, before you make a full confession?"

"Oh yes, I will spill my guts out for you completely."

Ellis turned to the mirror and smiled, then beckoned with his hand as he said, "Great. Your coffee'll be here real soon."

Behind the glass, Chief Paraquez was shaking her head. "Something doesn't feel right here," she said. "Why does he want to talk all of a sudden?"

One of the other female officials grumbled. "By God, he better not have finagled his way back out onto the street. If some greaseball lawyer shows up..."

"Here comes the coffee. Let's just see if he follows through on his promise."

The roomful of observers watched as a female duty officer entered the interrogation room and handed a disposable cup to Investigator Ellis. He waited for her to leave, then set the cup in front of the suspect.

They heard the man say, "Thank you," then saw him consult his watch again. He looked up at Ellis, who threw out his arms and said, "Well? I'm waiting."

The suspect's face bunched up. His right eye began twitching rapidly. Then his body lurched in a series of violent convulsions. He shot up from the chair, staggering to his right as he clutched at his chest and stomach.

Just as Ellis made a move to restrain him, the man leaned forward and vomited a horrendous stream of red and whitish slop across the room. Ellis flung himself away to avoid being drenched.

The sick man wobbled back against the far wall. He vomited again, with the mess now spilling all over his shirt and blazer as he slumped down onto the floor. A moment later his head drooped to the side and was still.

The observation room was in a panic.

"What the fuck just *happened?*"

"Is our suspect... dead?!"

"He didn't even touch the coffee..."

Detective Ashley Westgard thought she knew what had occurred.

"He took one," she said quietly.

"What do you mean by that?" Paraquez said.

"He took one of his own products. A terminator tasty."

"How? When? It definitely wasn't on our watch, not a chance."

"He probably had it in his breast pocket the whole time, just in case. As soon as he realized we were pouncing back at the tenement house, I bet that's when he swallowed it."

"Wait, wait," Paraquez said. "Why the hell would he say anything to us at all, if he knew it was only a matter of time before he died?"

Ash smiled. "Maybe it was a warning. Or an official corporate announcement."

"Jesus Fucking Christ!" another official yelled. The older man turned to Paraquez and added, "Get her out of here, right now. We are shutting this whole thing down."

Paraquez raised her eyebrows at Ash. "Detective Westgard, if you'll please?"

"What?!" Ash said. "Are you kidding me?"

"It's above your pay grade," the man said.

"No way! That was my collar." Ash was furious. "I helped save every one of your asses. And the city's too."

"Detective!" Paraquez said sternly. In a more diplomatic tone she added, "Yes, you absolutely helped facilitate the apprehension of a dangerous criminal. One hundred percent. Now walk away and take your victory lap. Because if you stick around for the fallout, you might get egg—or worse—on your face." She motioned to the messy scene in the interrogation room.

"Victory lap?" Ash said incredulously. "For what? This case didn't close. The way I see things, it just started. And I want in!"

"Detective Westgard," the senior official said gently. "I do believe you've only held that rank for less than two years. I've been in these trenches for nearly thirty. So take it from me. If you make a career in law enforcement, there'll be a hundred opportunities to get your hands—and your conscience—quite dirty."

"So there's nothing I can do or say to stop this... cover up?"

"I'm afraid not. Think back on the oath you took. Duty, hierarchy, obeying orders. These are crucially important. We've all got to accept our roles, otherwise the seams of society will completely rip apart."

Ash said, "Thirty years, huh? And this is where your mind lands?"

The man straightened his posture. "The weight of the world," he said. "So don't rush in, Detective. The fire won't burn itself out anytime soon. Your day will come."

"Understood, sir."

Ash shook his hand firmly and left the observation room without another word.

25. A MILLION NAUGHTY ELEPHANTS

"Hiya, kid."

Ash had found Vernon asleep on a bench outside the interview rooms. Now he opened his eyes and sat up.

"What are you still doing here?" she asked. "It's nearly morning. Waiting to give your statement, or—"

She flashed a smile, folding her arms as she struck a pose.

"Yeah," he said. "I didn't want to go home without... seeing you or saying goodbye."

"*Goodbye?* Come on, you! Let's get something to eat."

Ash lightly scratched his upper back as they walked down a wide-open hallway toward the exit.

All the nastiness and complicated stress she had carried out of that observation room, it just fell away the instant she rounded the corner and saw her favorite runt huddled under his jacket.

The little guy had risen to the ultimate occasion—one that was even more important than satisfying her, in fact. He had agreed to put his *life* on the line. And for her own part, Ash now felt a kind of appreciation and gratitude that she never had before.

Beyond having her demands submitted to by others... Beyond reciprocating sexual favors... Beyond admiring someone's physique or watching them bench press five hundred pounds... There lay a new realm where the feelings were richer and more enveloping, if not as frantic or thrilling as what she was used to.

Outside the station, she watched Vernon jump up onto her ATV like an old pro. After the raid, medical staff had checked him out before sending him back here in a squad car. Besides a few scrapes and bruises, he would come out of this ordeal no worse for wear. Unless, of course, Ash decided to give him a farewell roll in the hay.

Because she knew that this fling couldn't really last. For any number of her own reasons *why*. She vowed that she would let him down easy this time. Emotionally at least.

But he really was adorable to look at. She'd just have to see how things played out...

At a stop light she turned her head back and said, "Burgers okay?"

"Sure."

Ash pulled into an automated all-night drive-thru and tapped out their orders. When the food was ready, she handed Vernon the bag and zipped back into the road.

Next she stopped in front of a fancy off-white apartment building with blue accent lights. She hopped off and said, "Hold tight."

Vernon stayed on the rear seat and waited for five minutes. Ash came running out the front door carrying a backpack. "Here, put this on," she said.

Fifteen minutes later she rolled the ATV into a parking space and cut the engine.

"Bet you thought it was back to the Express Pod, yeah?" She smiled, offering her arm as they entered the lobby of a ritzy hotel. "Gimme a sec."

Again Vernon waited in silence, now marveling at the hotel's opulent interior.

Ash came back over with a wave. "Alrighty, let's head up!"

They took an elevator to the fifth floor, then Ash burst out as soon as the doors opened.

"Come on!" she called. "Catch up!"

Vernon ran down the hallway after her, turning right at a split, only to feel her crash into him and press her lips against his. Then she backed away and led him by the hand.

She unlocked one of the doors, stepping aside as she said, "After you, fine sir."

It was a beautiful suite, with beige walls and richly colored draperies. Vernon had never been anywhere so nice before.

They sat down on the living room rug and ate. She pulled a six-pack of beer out of her bag and cracked two cans open. "Cheers!"

"Cheers," Vernon said.

After they washed their hands at the kitchen sink, Ash trotted into the other room and dropped down on the bed. Vernon followed, then stood at the door waiting for her next command.

"Oh Vernon," she said, rolling onto her back and starting to untie one of her braids. "What are we going to do with you?"

"I know what *I* want." He stepped forward and leaned his knee onto a corner of the bed.

Ash felt his eyes move down the length of her body in anticipation. But she had a surprise in store for him...

She twisted onto her belly and said, "So, what do you think the lab's gonna pull out of that tasty you bought?"

"Nothing good," Vernon said. "Have the police even found the other two killers' bodies?"

"Not yet. But they could be anywhere. In an empty field. Floating in the river. Or a traffic fatality made to look like an accident..."

Vernon sighed. "Well, no one at home's said anything so far. But... you know how it is. They don't send alerts around town when we go missing."

"Aw, come on now. Don't start moping." She pulled him in for a kiss. "I only brought it up because I have a little treat for us that I picked up at home."

Ash reached into her pants pocket and pulled out a square plastic case. She handed it to Vernon.

"What is it?" he asked. "Not a tasty? I didn't know cops used."

"Puh-lease!" She gave a hearty laugh. "*Everybody* has secrets nowadays. A million naughty elephants crammed together in the same room, haha."

Vernon pried open the slim container with his fingernail. Two round black pills were held in place side by side. On the surface was a bit of computer jargon printed in gray:

C:

"Wait... is this Admin?"

She smiled. "Yes indeed. And I want to feel you inside me while we're on it."

"*Yeah?*"

"Oh yeah. Very much so, Mister Vernon. Now come on, let's get out of these clothes and take a shower. I want to be clean... before we get dirty!"

Ash and Vernon rose slowly, looking into each other's eyes as they swallowed the tasties. Their minds would soon experience the sensation of having godlike powers and unlimited access to the secrets of the universe. Just as they would merge into one while granting unlimited access to each other's bodies.

They disrobed and stepped into the steam and spray of a hot shower...

THE END.

If you enjoyed this story and would like to see
Ash's adventures continue, please visit the website
where you purchased the book and post a review.

ABOUT THE AUTHOR

Philip Wyeth is an entrepreneur, musician, film aficionado, heavy metal addict, and hockey fan. As a writer, his work includes short fiction and editorials. This is his fifth novel.

His website is www.philipwyeth.com. Follow him across the social media landscape under the following handles:

@PhilipWyeth: Twitter, BitChute, Gab, and Minds.

@PhilipWyethWriter: Instagram and Facebook.